Above the Clouds:
A Saga of Song

Nina Minsky

ISBN: 979-8-6385-1248-4

DEDICATION

Dedicated to my mother, Amanda Minsky, who was always there for me and believed in my writing. She was the only one I ever trusted to edit my work. She is forever loved and missed by me and my siblings.

CONTENTS

ACKNOWLEDGMENTS

I want to thank my best friend Collin for encouraging me to self-publish my book, and believing that it deserved to be published. I would also like to thank my boyfriend Jon for helping me prepare the book for publishing and letting me vent my frustration at him throughout this 6 year process.

1 CHAPTER ONE

It wasn't the job she'd wanted. She'd argued fiercely with Rahien, Angel of the North Star over it, everyone knew she wasn't the best fighter, that wasn't her strength. In the end Rahien had silenced her protests with nothing more than the stony glare he was so famous for and she'd been forced to bitterly admit defeat. She glimpsed the tumultuous mountain peaks of Eyria and with a resigned sigh prepared herself for the battle at hand. Quelling a giant's riot was never easy, and she knew better than to think she could reason with them.

Drawing her twin swords from the cross scabbard on her back she silently glided through the frigid air, every sense alert to the threat of sudden danger. Her opalescent wings cut through the dense fog surrounding the mountains with the same practiced ease as her swords cut through her opponents. Finally her feet reached ground and her wings vanished into her back, leaving behind nothing but a scared girl.

Not that she would ever be mistaken as merely a girl, or merely a human for that matter. There was something undeniably otherworldly about her, from her pale skin so luminescent it glowed, to her hair paler and finer than a tuft of cloud. Her deep violet eyes shown like amethysts, they were at once both frightening and radiant to behold. Inspiring, as so many artists had said of her over the years, a beauty so pure it could only have come from God. A God that had been absent for five hundred long years now, leaving his Angels to wander the world lost without purpose.

There was a light footstep behind her and she whirled, swords at the ready to see Lianzet, Angel of Storm coming to a graceful landing. He cocked his head at her, amber eyes shining with amusement.

"You intend to fight me?" he asked with a disarming smile.

"How could I ever bring harm to something so beautiful?" she replied, burying the tips of her swords into the soil.

Lianzet was beautiful, and he knew it. He had been the inspiration behind most of the Egyptian gods, with his golden skin and glorious long hair, blacker even than the sky on a night robbed of stars. His eyes were an intense warm gold, framed by lush dark eyelashes and tapered brow. He moved like a tiger, elegant and strong, powerful and dangerous but with a beauty that made you forget just how dangerous he really was.

"You followed me," She said pointedly, crossing her arms in what she hoped was an intimidating stance.

He merely chuckled, "Weren't you hoping that I would?"

Actually, she was sort of relieved to see him, though she'd never admit to that. As irritating as it was to have him tailing her like an overprotective parent, the sad truth was that she did need his protection. With him there she felt much safer taking on the unruly giants; Lianzet would never fall in battle.

She ignored his question, "What of your mission? Did escorting a holy man to Thiatmar prove too difficult a task for you?"

He raised an eyebrow, "Come now Asielle, you know me better than that. I would not be here had I not completed my mission. When I returned it was to find that you had been dispatched to this frozen wasteland. Why Halliel insists on giving you the most dangerous missions I will never understand. You clearly have need of my assistance, and so I came."

Halliel…she scowled in spite of herself, how she hated that narcissistic fool. Soon after God's initial disappearance, Halliel had declared himself the commander and had been ordering them all about ever since. Of course, he had been challenged many times in those first chaotic months, but Halliel was a merciless fighter, and he had felled every challenger with a brutality that made Asielle sick to her stomach. Of all the Angels, Lianzet was probably the only one who could triumph in a battle with Halliel, but Lianzet had no pretensions of leadership and though he had not exactly bowed his head in allegiance he had not contested either.

Asielle knew very well why Halliel always sent her on the missions with the least likelihood of success. He'd never forgiven her for refusing his advances over a half-century ago. The guy really knew how to hold a grudge.

"Asielle?" Lianzet's smooth, dark tone broke into her reverie. "Shouldn't we be going?"

"Ah…of course," she said, embarrassed by her lack of focus, especially in front of Lianzet, whose mind was always focused solely on the task at hand and who would never be caught dead daydreaming in the field of battle.

She trudged along behind Lianzet, who had wordlessly taken the lead, musing to herself, as she quite often did, how unsuited she was for this life. Why had God ever made her an Angel? Unlike her peers, she was not assigned to anything specific, even before the war she had not had a duty that she alone was to perform. She'd worn many guises over the millennium, Angel of the Night Sky, Angel of Summer Breezes, but never anything permanent, there was no birthright for her to claim, no inherent place that she belonged. It'd always bothered her, why out of all the Angels, she alone had no explicit purpose. Was there a secret one that God had not yet revealed to her? Or was she simply there as a substitute for Angels that had been assigned a purpose?

She bumped into Lianzet, startled, as she always was, by the warmth of him. The touch of his bare skin was shocking, like sticking your hand into a fire. She'd asked him once before why he wasn't the Angel of Fire, a title that had been bequeathed to his brother. He'd chuckled and stated that he simply wasn't chaotic enough to be fire. It'd made a strange sort of sense, Lianzet was fearsome but always well-composed, and he lacked the rebellious streak and penchant for chaos that his younger brother Tearin was so known for.

"Stay close." Lianzet said with a grin, causing her to blush with shame, "We've found them."

Peering over his shoulder she could see the hulking shoulders of the giants, covered in thick moss and craggy boulders so that to the untrained eye it looked as though the mountain itself was moving. It was an easy mistake to make; the beasts were the size of small mountains after all. The only obvious difference was their furnace-like eyes that glowed in the deep pits of their sockets like hellfire. There was nothing but a lazy sort of intelligence behind those eyes, no hint of a soul or gist of camaraderie. That's what made the giants such loathsome beings, at least to her mind. They had no fealty, no respect for the sacredness of life, which is why in eons past; God had been forced to cow them into submission.

Before that interference, the giants had roamed the world freely, leaving blazing paths of destruction in their wake. The wars between the colossal beasts had stymied the growth of human civilization and laid waste to the land. They had been cast into a cursed slumber and forbidden to exist alongside humans, though ironically many human abodes had been built upon their slumbering forms. Several of these giants boasted small huts on their backs as if they were trophies and Asielle wondered what had happened to their unfortunate inhabitants.

There was no need to wonder, of course, there was only one possible outcome for a human confrontation with giants, and it wasn't pleasant. With a sinking sensation stinging her gut she realized that the fire currently burning bright in the giant's eyes most likely came from the souls they had consumed.

"Disgusting creatures…" she murmured under her breath.

"Mmm." Lianzet agreed. "Indeed they are. Now, my sweet songbird, where would you first strike?" He looked at her appraisingly.

"I am not your student." She said huffily, resentful of his condescending tone.

"And yet, there is much you could learn from me. Much you *should* learn from me, for I will not always be around to protect you." He said, suddenly solemn.

"And where would you go?" she retorted. "It's not as though you'll ever die." She regretted the harshness of those words as soon as they left her mouth but it was too late to retrieve them.

Lianzet's face remained inscrutable.

"I hope for your sake, that that day never comes."

What would it take to kill an Angel? She wondered, as she reached out to take Lianzet's hot hand in hers. "Yes, I hope so too." She said, squeezing his hand softly by way of apology.

He smiled at her and gave her a gentle squeeze back. As always, she was forgiven. Lianzet had never been able to stay mad at her for long, for which she was most grateful. She had only seen Lianzet truly, viciously angry once, and it was a sight she hoped to never see again. For years it had haunted her dreams, turning them into horrific nightmares. She was one of the few Angels who had the luxury to dream, though she hadn't been appreciative of it then. And how cruel she'd felt, when she awoke screaming in terror only to see Lianzet's concerned face and cowered away from him in a fear he had never given her any reason for. How hurt he'd been, though he'd tried not to show it, always playing the part of the strong older brother, though she was not of his family.

"There's something wrong." She surmised, eying the giants as they milled aimlessly about. "It's far too quiet. Why aren't they fighting? I was expecting mayhem."

"It is quite puzzling." Lianzet responded, confirming her suspicion. "Perhaps there is a leader unseen, an instigator of this said rebellion."

"A leader…But who? Who could organize the giants? They have respect for no one."

"Well, they are awake. That much of the report was accurate. They must not be allowed to remain sentient, they are far too unpredictable." He summoned his scythe to his side and twirled it expertly. If giants were capable of feeling fear, they would certainly fear the wrath of this imposing Angel.

He winked at her. "Are you ready?"

"But there are so many of them…"

"Do you doubt me?"

"No…never. I only doubt myself…"

"Asielle, you must never doubt yourself." He said brusquely. "I know that your talent lies far from the battlefield, but there is no other I would bring with me to this fight."

He was lying of course, but she felt her spirit lift in spite of that. She may not be a warrior, but neither was she completely useless in battle. As quietly as she could manage she began to sing softly, her notes weaving around their weapons like vines, fortifying them with mystical strength. The dulcet tones spread to their bodies, causing them to glow with a strength borrowed from the Heavens. It may not be much, but it was the best she could do at such low volume.

Lianzet smiled at her encouragingly, "That's my girl." He said fondly. "Now let's put those giants back in dreamland where they belong."

She rose with him and in a flash they were on the harsh slope of the battlefield, surrounded by gargantuan beasts as old as time and cruel and callous as aging. They didn't take long to notice their presence and began flailing their massive limbs in an attempt to crush them. They leapt fleetly out of the way, nimbly dodging the giant's clumsy attacks. Luckily their massive size was not matched with speed; giants were slow-witted and equally slow of movement.

Lianzet's scythe came down with blinding speed and a giant roared in pain as his arm broke loose from his body and smacked into the ground, causing the earth to well up around it in a furrow. The giant's blue blood filled the field, stealing the life from every plant it touched and scorching the ground. The Angels took care to avoid it, knowing full well how toxic it was. It lacked the power necessary to kill them, but the pain of its contact with skin was excruciating.

Lianzet sprung onto the bloody stump where the giant's arm had previously resided and swung his scythe with fearsome might into the giant's skull. The giant collapsed to the ground with a scream of fury, its smoldering eyes glowing faintly as embers before sputtering out completely.

One down. Asielle eyed the nearest giant, determined to do her part. This giant was slightly more evolved than the others, and was flinging large boulders at her from atop a ridge. Asielle ran at him, keeping a careful eye on the shadows that fell on the ground, precursors to the boulder's inevitable landing. What she lacked in strength, Asielle made up for in speed and agility. It did not take her long to reach the giant's side, and she dug her twin blades into the creature's back, using all her might to break through the scaly surface.

The skin of a giant was impenetrable to any man-made weapon, only a weapon of Heaven could pierce their tough hide. The giant grunted in agitation and reached a massive hand behind it to try and grasp the culprit. Asielle bounded up its spine; using one of her twin swords for leverage for her feet she vaulted onto the beast's head and dug her second blade into the giant's crag of an eye.

Blue blood spewed forth as the giant crashed head-first into a tree and then crumbled to the ground. Asielle looked for Lianzet, proud of her accomplishment, but he was busy engaging two more of the fiends. *There is no time for pride in the heat of battle.* She reminded herself, and turned to face another giant who was galloping towards her, its feet like gnarled tree branches causing the whole mountain to shake with such force she feared an avalanche.

Several weary battles later, the mountain slope was devoid of all life other than two exhausted Angels. Asielle slumped to the ground by Lianzet's side, gazing in horror at the destruction they had wrought. The mountain was a dead thing, covered in ghastly blue, with the remnants of charred plant life mixed in. Not a tree was left standing, and everywhere were lifeless mounds of rock that had before been living creatures. Even the snow that had begun to fall evaporated upon contact with the blue blood, nothing more than a hiss of steam to prove that it had ever existed.

Lianzet knelt beside her, and she waited, expecting a compliment for her hard-fought victories, but instead he frowned at her and shook his head with a mixture of disapproval and concern.

"You were careless, Asielle." He said, holding his palm out to touch her porcelain arm.

"What? But I---" she followed his gaze and saw the thick stream of silver blood oozing from the gash in her arm. She hadn't even noticed she'd been hit.

"It's a pity it won't scar. A scar might remind you to not be so reckless in the future." He commented, as healing light spread from his body to the wound.

"Hmph. One itty-bitty wound, I'd say that's pretty impressive."

"No wounds would be far more impressive."

She sighed, Lianzet was frugal with compliments. A glint in a pile of rubble that had been a giant's head caught her eye and she floated over to inspect it.

"Asielle…"

"Lianzet…there's something here. Something…not right." She dug a shiny metal fragment out of the rock and examined it, it was about as long as her palm, made not of silver but of Uthicon, a magically endowed metal known only to the gods and their vassals. It bore a small symbol, crudely cut but unmistakable, the mark of I'rae.

Lianzet took it from her hand and stared at it solemnly.

"So…it was the I'rae who were controlling the giants. This is far more complicated than a simple rebellion…this is an act of war."

War with the I'rae. It was of course inevitability, they'd all known it would come to this, but Asielle had never dreamed she'd be a part of it, and yet here she was, on a mountain bathed in blood, with a declaration of war staring her in the face. Her mind froze in panic as visualizations of future bloody battles paralyzed her brain.

"Damn it." Was all she could say.

2 CHAPTER TWO

The Hallowed Cloister was empty when they finally made it back home, their footsteps echoing as loud as dragon thunder on the sleek marbled floors. Asielle felt a sense of relief wash over her, as welcoming as hot water after a long, cold day. She was glad to be back, she always felt at her safest when nestled away here in Itsukuenel, the Holy City. As if nothing could ever breach the sanctity of that floating fortress, impenetrable in its constant shield of clouds. This would always be her sanctuary, the only home she had ever known, or cared to remember.

All the other Angels must be away on missions, she had never seen it so empty. If she hadn't known better she would have assumed the place was deserted, nothing but the occasional shed feather as proof that anything living had ever existed in this place. She looked to Lianzet for guidance but he was eerily silent. He hadn't spoken the entire flight back, and the fact that he was so disturbed by their discovery frightened her. She had never seen even the faintest glimmer of fear in Lianzet's eyes, and though he did not appear fearful there was a definite crack in his normally inscrutable façade.

She knew, of course, that war of any kind was a big deal, and definite cause for worry. However, Lianzet's sudden grimness gave her pause. It had not occurred to her that a battle with the I'rae might be a battle they could lose. It was beyond her imagination to even consider Lianzet's noble visage bowed in defeat. And if they were to lose the world to the I'rae…then the light of the world would be sealed away forever.

She shuddered at the thought and glued herself to Lianzet's side as he strode with a sense of divine purpose through the Hall of Light towards the Judgment Chamber. Asielle found herself hoping that Halliel would not be there, perched in his customary seat in the place of judging; as if by keeping their newfound discovery to themselves, they could somehow delay the oncoming war. Of course, he was there, as she'd known deep in her heart that he would be. Halliel very rarely left the Holy City Itsukuenel, unless there was a particularly bloody mission on the table. Sometimes Asielle wasn't sure what it was that kept Halliel from crossing over and becoming one of the I'rae, he certainly had the same penchant for bloodshed, the same fiendish delight in destruction.

After all, that's all the I'rae really were, renegade Angels who had cut ties to Itsukuenel and their silent God and embraced the darkest parts of their souls. They were not demons. Though Daemons were real, the demons humans believed in had never existed, just as there had never been any truth to Hell or the Devil. These were just fictitious creations of the human mind, born of a need to satisfy their craving of right and wrong. The moral compasses of some humans were so very weak that they required the belief that punishment followed wrongdoing. In truth, God rarely inflicted punishment, and usually for sins far greater than most mortals were capable of devising. Not that God did not have a vengeful side, anyone who had ever met an Angel knew that they were capable of far more than soft beauty, they were built as instruments of God's will, enforcers of the highest degree. There were few laws that God held sacred above all else, and these were not to be ignored. For those offenders, punishment was swift and severe and the elite of the elite were called upon to ensure God's justice was served.

The Angels of Redemption were the supreme guard dogs of Heaven, acting independently to fulfill their sacred mission they were rarely seen by the lesser Angels and never socialized with them. These were the Angels of ancient times, when darkness and despair ruled the land and God's judgment had seared the earth. They were battle-hardened creatures, not one without scars, both real and imagined. In the recent eras of peace there had been no real need for these bloody Angels, and they'd disappeared into the annals of history. Asielle knew that they were still out there, carrying out their mission even in the absence of God's word. There were no Daemons left to fight, but evil came in many forms and there could never exist a world without the taint of its presence.

Daemons had existed once, before God had used his mighty wrath to bring order to the chaotic land, but now all that remained of them were shadows and legends. They had been foul spirits, beings of darkness that lived in the byways of light whose sole purpose in being was to cause chaos and destruction. They came in many forms, any creature who shunned light long enough became demon in both name and form. The shadows of daemons were referred to as Fiends, and they were capable of nothing more than petty crimes and occasionally turning a particularly suggestive mind towards evil. Asielle had tangled with them before in the past, mere echoes of their evil source. A Fiend was nothing compared to the fury of a warring Angel.

"Well…returned from our missions already, have we?" Halliel inquired from his carved wooden throne with an air of offensive incredulity. Clearly he was expecting a report of failure.

Lianzet would not favor him with a bow and with him beside her Asielle felt a rash braveness creep over her and did not let her head dip into its customary acknowledgment of respect. Halliel noticed and a scowl formed on his face, maiming his otherwise handsome features. There was no such thing as an unfortunate looking Angel, and Halliel was no exception. He was of Olympian stature, rippled with sinewy muscles that betrayed the femininity of his face. Fine golden curls hung in perfect ringlets around his chiseled features, square jaw and aquiline nose adorned his perfectly symmetrical face. Piercing blue eyes peered out at her from lowered lashes of downy white gold. She looked away uncomfortably, feeling the weight of his intense stare.

"Halliel. We succeeded in quelling the giant's rebellion but there is more to the situation than we surmised."

"Care to tell me what it was you were doing in Eyria, Lianzet? That was not the mission you were assigned. It was to be Asielle's mission, and hers alone. I do not need one of my most valuable fighters tied up with such a trivial job."

"Who cares why he was there? What does it matter as long as we got the job done?" Asielle blurted out, shocked at her brashness.

Halliel shot her an icy glare that sent her heart scampering for cover.

"Quiet, Asielle. If I want your opinion, I will ask it."

Oh how she hated that pretentious cur, what right had he to sit there in judgment? She visualized scratching that self-righteous smirk off his flawless face to placate her anger.

"You know better than to assign such a dangerous mission to Asielle, it pushes the limits of her abilities to throw her into such a volatile situation. Without my assistance I doubt she would've escaped unscathed. But perhaps that was what you were hoping for…Halliel?"

Lianzet's voice was a low, predatory growl; he was taking a stand, no more perilous missions for Asielle. Halliel didn't even flinch, but he backed down nonetheless, he knew better than to make an enemy of Lianzet.

"Of course not, I would be as distraught as you if some harm were to befall our ravishing comrade. Perhaps you are right, I may have overestimated her capabilities, though had I known you'd come rushing to her aid I would have assigned her a far more difficult task."

"I did not abandon my post. My mission was successfully completed; I simply thought the most efficient course was for me to assist Asielle with hers." There was no arguing with his flat tone.

Halliel stretched and stood on the dais that supported his throne, his 6'6 frame all the more imposing with its added height. Arms folded he surveyed the two Angels before him as if they were some sort of exotic cargo delivered for his inspection.

"And so? What news do you bring? What is of such importance as to bring the exalted Lianzet to my humble abode?" he said with a sinister smirk.

Lianzet seemed oblivious to the challenge in Halliel's words and simply opened up his hand to reveal the signet.

"This."

Halliel quite grumpily left the grandeur of his perch to take a closer look at the curious object nestled in Lianzet's bronzed palm. His golden brows narrowed into a furrow as realization crept across the pristine pools of his eyes.

"Where did you find this?" He demanded, snatching it from Lianzet's hand and holding it up to the light.

"Asielle was the one to find it, embedded in the skulls of the giants. It seems the I'rae were behind their sudden rebellion."

"Of course…their movements seemed unnaturally coordinated, I should've guessed at the I'rae's involvement. So, did they plan to draw us out with this ploy? Or are they merely flexing their powers? Either way, they cannot be allowed such freedom of movement; their taunts must be answered with force. Those brutes understand nothing else."

He returned to his throne, the metal shard clutched so tightly in his clenched fist that blood seeped out from between the knuckles. His obvious fury rippled through the air like a heat wave and giggling to herself Asielle wondered how the hot-head's hair didn't burn right off. Lianzet shot her a reprimanding look and she stifled her laughter, chastened.

"Thank you for bringing this to my attention Lianzet, you have done well. This requires immediate action, and I will see to it that appropriate measures are taken."

There was an air of dismissal in his voice and it did not fail to escape Lianzet's notice.

"Very well then, we shall excuse ourselves." Lianzet headed towards the door, gesturing to Asielle to follow.

"And Lianzet, this…'discovery' of yours does not leave this room, is that understood? There is no need to cause a panic quite yet."

Lianzet did not even break his stride as he responded.

"Yes of course, I understand."

"Asielle…you stay." Halliel added, freezing her in her tracks. She looked at Lianzet pleadingly but he shrugged and gave her an apologetic smile, she was on her own.

The door closed behind him and she turned around slowly, her mind racing with endless and frightful possibilities. What could Halliel possibly have to say to her? Did he intend to berate her for accepting help on her mission? The Judgment room was aptly named, deep and dark like a dug-out pit natural light struck only one part of the room, the throne, bathing

Halliel in a glow of heavenly light while leaving the judged in bitter darkness. She shifted her feet uncomfortably, wishing Halliel would speak instead of subjecting her to this insufferable silence but he just sat there, scrutinizing every detail of her face as silver blood dripped onto the claws of his throne.

"Have you nothing to say, then?" she asked, fed up with waiting.

He chuckled and like a graceful, long-legged egret floated down to stand in front of her, the shadows doing nothing to take away from his magnificent yet treacherous beauty.

"Will you disappoint me again, the sweetest of my Angels?" he asked, circling her slowly as a lion circles its unsuspecting prey.

"Your Angels? We belong to no one but God." She answered, rebelliousness sparking in her amethyst eyes.

"I don't know if you've noticed but…God is quite absent." Halliel retorted, reaching out a hand and boldly twisting one of Asielle's silver strands around his finger, and roughly pulling it towards him, effectively yanking her face closer to his.

"Don't you touch me!" she fumed, her veins crackling with lightening as she jerked out of his grasp.

"Really…how long must you fight me, Asielle?" he asked with a sigh, as if her refusal was becoming tiring. "The sooner you accept my…proposal, the sooner we can move past this nastiness between us."

"The sooner you give up…the sooner I can stop hating you." She fired back.

He snorted with derision. "You will cave to my desires, my lovely Asielle. Or do you intend to cower behind Lianzet for the rest of eternity? Surely he grows tired of protecting you from me."

"Find another." She protested, knowing it was a weak argument. Halliel was not one to accept defeat, much as she'd hoped he would, his pride would not allow him to forget the sting of her rebuttal. Nausea crept into her lungs, filling her every breath with the knowledge that Halliel would never be satisfied until he'd won this war between them. She wondered if it was even about her anymore, or was it simply a matter of pride now?

"Why should I, when you are the only one who tastes so sweet?" With a deftness that astounded her, Halliel moved into her, pressing his unwanted lips against hers, tapered fingers clawing at her hair. For one horrible second she was frozen with shock, her brain racing to make sense of what had just happened. Halliel's lips curled into a self-satisfied smile against her skin, sensing her powerlessness and assured of his eventual victory.

Her foot stomped down on his with a force that would have shattered a mortal's bones and he let out a small, surprised yelp as he pulled away from her. His wings flared out behind him, summoned by his anger, creating a fearsome sight.

"You…" he spat, a guttural growl rising in his throat. "You will live to regret that, my dear." He used the endearment like a threat, and she thought for a moment that he might strike her but instead he chuckled harshly. "No matter how you struggle, you will be with me, Asielle…" he said, the cracks in his confidence receding.

She backed into the shadows, wanting to hide her fear from him, though she knew he could sense it, like a scent on the breeze.

"You may go." He said, waving a hand dismissively.

Forcing her feet not to run she walked with as much composure as she could muster towards the heavy oaken door, pushing it open with veritable ease, though it would've taken twenty men to budge it. Once in the halls however, away from his scornful laugh, she allowed her feet to give in to instinct and ran, her feet so fleet they barely touched ground. She ran right past Lianzet, who had been waiting for her propped up against the wall, past the Hallway of Effulgent Light and into the Courtyard of Memories past which the dormitories lay. Tears of frustration had sprung unbidden to her eyes and she frantically brushed them away as she ran, not wanting anyone to see her so emotional.

*I'm weak, so weak…*she thought as she flung open her dormitory door and threw herself upon her bed, spun from unicorn's dreams. Her tears seeped into the cloud-like material and dripped through to the ground. *None of the other Angels ever cry…*

A timid knock came on the door and she knew without thought that it was Lianzet come to check on her. Feeling sorry for herself she refused the promise of kindness that his presence offered and buried her face so deep in her bed that she could not hear his patient entreaties.

What am I to do?

3 CHAPTER THREE

When she awoke from her tear-soaked sleep her fair skin was covered in finely beaded moonlight causing her skin to glisten and glow like newly fallen snow. It felt to her like a blessing from above and she smiled at the sight. Her dreams had been filled with a strange, impermeable fog so thick that it felt like water in her lungs. She'd awoken choking and sputtering for breath several times only to drift back into a restless slumber once the panic dissipated. It was an omen, she was sure of it, here there was no such thing as just a dream, to dream at all meant something. She had no need to feel curious about this latest dream. Doubtless it had something to do with the impending war with the I'rae, which was certainly a catastrophe in her mind. Perhaps the I'rae had some other foul surprise lying in wait for the Angels to discover. An ambush, or a rebellion amongst the Darklings, the strange little whisp-like creatures of Shadowlight that inhabited the Underneath of Earth. Whatever it was, she refused to be taken off-guard.

Rising from bed she reached for the door, ready to face whatever this new day may have in store for her. As she opened it, Lianzet tumbled into the room and she realized he must have been leaning up against it. He grinned sheepishly up at her, flat on his back on the floor.

"Have you been there all night?" she inquired, knowing he'd deny it.

"Don't be absurd." He answered, getting to his feet in one smooth, liquid movement.

"Oh I'm the absurd one, am I? I'm not the one who was sleeping against a door all night." She said, giving him an amused smile.

"Asielle..." his tone of voice changed and became suddenly solemn. "Are you alright? What happened last night?"

She laughed lightly, trying to brush it off. "You know Halliel has a way of getting under my skin, I'm quite alright I assure you."

"I wish you wouldn't lie to me." He replied, and she felt as though she'd just been slapped in the face.

"Lie? But I..."

Lianzet held his hand out to her, palm unfurled to reveal dozens of exquisite, flawless opals, each in the perfect shape of a teardrop. Asielle colored visibly as she recognized her handiwork. She'd tried to catch her tears before they fell and solidified into opals but several had escaped during her hurried flight. She hung her head in shame.

"I…I'm sorry Lianzet. I didn't want to worry you."

"I'm already worried. So tell me, what has upset you so?" He laid a comforting hand upon her shoulder and she leaned into his warmth gratefully.

"Halliel still hopes to entrap me."

Lianzet sighed. "I was afraid of that. That stubborn fool has never conceded defeat in the entirety of his miserable existence. I should never have left you alone with him."

Surprised at the guilt in his voice Asielle favored him with the sweetest smile she could muster.

"Come now, we were both of us powerless to refuse his order. He will doubtless keep finding ways to get me alone; I shouldn't let it bother me so."

"Perhaps I should lay claim to you myself." He said, his expression inscrutable.

"Wha-what??" Asielle stammered, more shocked than she cared to admit.

He grinned at her roguishly and she relaxed, realizing he hadn't been serious.

"Enough of this foolishness. We have a mission."

"Oh?" she said, her curiosity piqued.

"Mm it's a bit dull, really. We're to go to the Callion Library to protect the Sacred Scrolls. Halliel seems to think that the I'rae may have interest in acquiring them."

"And Halliel requested that you take me along? I thought he didn't want us working together."

"I don't want you alone with him. You're safest with me."

She giggled, *so Halliel had nothing to do with this decision.* Before Halliel had become such a problem she'd thought Lianzet's over-protectiveness quite annoying. He'd always fought to make sure she was given the safest missions, when he'd allowed her to partake in them at all that is. Used to be he wouldn't let her leave the shelter of the Holy City at all without an escort. How many times had he forced his younger brother Tearin to accompany her on her visits to the Isles to pick flowers or to watch the annual migration of the pegasi? Tearin was quite the firebrand and had protested fiercely of course, but he had yet to win a battle of wits against his brother and he was always forced to secede. He made for poor company, constantly complaining and just generally being as belligerent as possible but he had always kept her safe.

Now in these times of strife Lianzet's over-protectiveness felt like a blessing. She certainly felt more at ease with him by her side, he would sooner die than let any harm befall her.

"Well then, shall we get going?" she said with a smile.

He merely nodded and led the way to the Moonrise Stable. Here Zelasemel tended to the Stars, brightly burning steeds engulfed in constant ice-blue fire and manes of silvery flame. This was the Angels preferred method of transportation when available but Zelasmel was stingy with lending them out and would have preferred to let them run free in the ebony skies. However she couldn't deny them their purpose, every star that shot across the night sky carried an angel on an errand. She didn't even acknowledge their entrance as she filled the marble basins with the comet dust the Stars consumed for food.

"Zelasmel, have you been well? I never see you outside of the stables."

"What reason is there for me to leave here?" she asked, standing to face them. She had the golden eyes of a panther and light emerald hair that was always tucked up into an impeccable bun. Her gossamer wings shimmered behind her in the faint light of the stables.

"You've come to borrow a Star I suppose, not to be social."

"Yes if it would not be too much trouble we have a mission in Callion, it is quite far to fly."

"Work order?" she requested, holding her hand out as gold-rimmed spectacles materialized on the bridge of her narrow nose.

Lianzet handed her the scrap of paper with Halliel's signature on it and she scrutinized it closely looking for possible reasons to dismiss their request. She scrunched her nose and looked up at them.

"It does seem that YOU have a mission in Callion, Lianzet, but it makes no mention of Asielle accompanying you." She said with a sniff.

"An oversight I'm sure." Lianzet said smoothly

"Halliel is normally quite thorough. I simply cannot release two of my Stars into your custody just so you can take Asielle on a romantic ride." She said with a pointed glare at Asielle, as if the whole thing had been her idea.

"I would never ask you to disobey Halliel. I will carry out my mission regardless of your cooperation, even if I must fly there. Asielle has gracefully offered to help me with my task, and that is why she stands here beside me, and for that reason alone."

Zelasmel sighed and it was clear she meant to acquiesce.

"Very well Lianzet, I trust in your intentions. However I am afraid I can only offer you what the work order grants you, which is one Star."

"That should be adequate; Asielle takes up very little space."

"This way please." Zelasmel led them to the summoning platform, a circular crystalline platform floating amidst the sea of clouds. She raised the gem-encrusted whistle from the chain around her neck and put it to her peach lips. A high-pitched whistle resonated around the heavens, a sound out of the range of hearing for mortals, and so brutally shrill that the Angels covered their ears in pain.

There was a distant whinny and a Star galloped into sight, skin covered in a thin sheet of ice from the coldness of the atmosphere. It pranced up to the platform and gazed at Zelasmel expectantly. She reached out a hand to stroke its opalescent nose and offered it a piece of amber which the Star nibbled on gratefully.

"Take good care of him, Lianzet. I expect him back by noon on the morrow."

Lianzet nodded in acknowledgment and mounted the beast in one fluid motion.

"Yes of course, he is in good hands Zelasmel, you have my thanks. Come, Asielle." He reached down a hand and Asielle grabbed hold as he pulled her atop the Star's broad back.

"Be sure to hold on tight." He cautioned as she wrapped her arms around his waist.

"Oh Lianzet, as if I haven't ridden upon a Star before." She replied with a toss of her head.

He chuckled. "I can trust you not to fall off, then? If you do, I won't bother to retrieve you."

Asielle pretended to act horrified, though they both knew he would never leave her behind. Lianzet whispered their destination into the Star's pointed ears and with a nod of its magnificent head it turned and cantered into the fading daylight. The speed of the Stars was incredible, from the Earth below it was merely a streak of silver light in the dark endless black of the sky, but the pace seemed even more incredible from atop its back. Moving so quickly that the other stars fixed in one position disappeared completely from sight and all that could be seen was black rushing by. It seemed like merely a blink of the eye and they had landed atop the roof of the Callion Library.

Lianzet dismounted and helped Asielle down, dismissing the Star to graze nearby until their mission was complete. The library was an impressive building in its own right, tall columns supported the weight of the intricate stain-glass ceiling, and vines of ivy twisted their way throughout the structure. A worn cobblestone path led up to the grand marble doors, carved with scenes from battles of the before time, beautiful Angels engaged in never-ending battles with monsters long since gone from this world. They approached the doors and they groaned open before them, sensing their holy presence.

Inside it was inexplicably bright, lit by magic spells enacted in eons past and still functioning. The smell of musty tomes filled the air though it looked as if the library had been built only yesterday so pristine were the floors and shelves. It was a place of magic, it held more books and tomes than could be seen, and more floors than should have been possible. While it appeared to be just one large room with vaulted oak ceilings, the doors at the end of every corridor led to whole other universes.

"So just how long are we supposed to sit here guarding the Sacred Scrolls?" Asielle asked as they walked silently through the room.

"Halliel wants them brought above where they can be more easily protected."

"Of course he does…He probably just wants to read them himself and obtain the power of a god." She said with a frustrated sigh.

The Sacred Scrolls were ancient documents possessing incredible destructive power. They had been created in a time before God and some Angels believed that it was these very scrolls that had granted God his powers. Why they hadn't been destroyed long ago to stop wars from being waged over them Asielle had never quite understood. She was certain they were destructible; after all they were just made of velum, weren't they?

"Would you rather they fall into Olucard's possession?"

Olucard was the leader of the resistance, head of the I'rae, the one responsible for corrupting once pure Angels into mercenaries for hire. The I'rae took on any horrid mission that was assigned to them, be it by demi-gods or mortal Kings. Most of the Angel's work consisted of cleaning up after the I'rae's bloody campaigns.

"No of course not, imagine what Olucard could do with that kind of power!" she shuddered at the thought and clung close to Lianzet as they approached what seemed to be just part of the stone wall. Pressing his palm against the wall a soft bluish light radiated outwards and seeped into the mortar between the stones. The wall shimmered in and out of existence and the cutout of a door appeared. The Angels walked through and the wall solidified behind them, as if it had never been anything but seamless.

4 CHAPTER FOUR

Ephremael watched from the shadows atop one of the bookshelves as Lianzet and Asielle disappeared beyond the wall. Their presence would make his job a bit more complicated but he was confident of his success regardless. He recognized the tall bronzed Angel as Lianzet, the Angel of Storm, but he had never before seen the slender Maiden of Heaven that accompanied him.

With the fleetness of a nighthawk he glided down between the bookshelves, his winged shadow a fearsome sight as if the Angel of Death himself was descending to collect. His crimson hair shone in the multi-colored light, a darker red than even a ruby could muster, which faded to an almost-black brown in the shadows. A red so dark as to only be seen when the light glinted off of it, revealing the living fire beneath. His turquoise eyes glistened fiercely, both deceptively calm and tumultuous, as if a storm lay in wait just below the surface. He was devastatingly handsome, yet undeniably intimidating. He was the sort of man whose unearthly beauty was enough to ensnare a woman's heart, but also the kind of man who looked as though he took a certain kind of pleasure in breaking them.

He reached into the pocket of his long black coat and took out what at first glance appeared to be nothing more than a small clay totem. Measuring less than three inches high it was a grotesque imp-like creature with beady jet-black eyes and crooked claws. Ephremael lifted the tiny clay figure up to his lips and blew softly in its face. The imp sputtered to life, its eyes alight with inherent mischief as it wrapped its grubby paws around Ephremael's slender fingers and dug its hundreds of tiny razor-sharp teeth in, eager to fulfill its hunger for destruction.

"Why you little---" he grabbed the little fiend's throat twixt forefinger and thumb and squeezed until the imp ceased its maniacal laughter and stared at him intently.

"Now listen here, I have a little job for you. I want you to tear this library apart, wreak havoc, make all the noise your dastardly little heart desires, just don't get caught. Understand?"

The imp nodded gleefully and Ephremael cautiously released it, never sure how capable of understanding the creatures were. It jumped from his hand to the floor and scampered off and soon he could see it whirling about like a screaming dervish, admitting a piercing scream of pride as books and torn pages flew through the air. Ephremael cloaked himself in shadows until he was hidden completely from sight and waited.

Asielle

A dreadful howl cut through the stillness in the air and Asielle stiffened with the anticipation of a fight. The Sacred Scrolls lay in a ghostly-lit chamber behind them, still sealed by Holy magic, seemingly accessible yet tantalizingly out of reach.

Lianzet shifted his stance and summoned his scythe.

"So, the intelligence was correct. They must have followed in our wake. I should have been more vigilant."

Asielle drew her twin blades and started for the door but Lianzet blocked her path.

"No. You stay here. Guard the Scrolls."

"But you may have need of me---"

"It may be a ploy to get us to leave the Scrolls unattended. There are two of us here for a reason. Protecting the Scrolls is of the utmost importance."

"And what of your safety? Is that not also important?" she asked stubbornly.

He laughed and ruffled her hair playfully, which only served to infuriate her further.

"You worry too much mon petit cherie. I'll be fine, as I always am."

"Maybe you don't worry enough." She grumbled.

He smiled. "The I'rae have no fighters who can match me in battle. I assure you I will return shortly."

Lianzet turned and left the secret passage, leaving Asielle to fume in solitude.

"How can he be so careless?? He thinks nothing of his own safety but God forbid he lets me do anything even remotely dangerous! He'd take on all the I'rae at once if he thought it would spare me from fighting. Sometimes he's so noble that I…that I just want to smack him! I wish he'd accept his own vulnerability and take help when it is offered." She sighed and sheathed her swords, frustrated. She paced back and forth in front of the Scrolls with their imperceptible barrier.

What were to happen if the barrier was to be contested? Seeing no sign of its existence made it hard to believe it was there, but Asielle knew that many things existed beyond sight and beyond the sense. There were whole worlds unseen by most, and they were just as real as the ones that could be seen. Still, she was curious. Would an alarm sound? Would ancient guardians be summoned from some otherworldly plane to punish the trespasser? Or perhaps the building itself would come to fevered life and destroy all those who threatened its sanctity.

She heard a shrill scream emanating from beyond the wall, in the caverns of the library. Though she knew it wasn't Lianzet who'd screamed, a sense of panic still gripped at her heart and she ran towards the concealed door, intent on lending Lianzet her help whether he wanted it or not.

Ephremael

Ephremael watched with a quiet delight as the imp turned the once serene library into a place of living chaos. Books were clawed to shreds, the shelves were knocked over like dominoes and the scent of imp piss lay thick in the air. The rank smell was too much for Ephremael's delicate senses and he covered his nose in disgust. He saw Lianzet emerge from the illusory wall and stalk down the aisle in search of the perpetrator of all this chaos, and he smiled with grim satisfaction. His ploy had worked.

As stealthily as the night creeps over the day Ephremael moved, one with the shadows as he made his way to the wall and with a faint brush of his hand released the binding spell. He stepped through into the darkness and collided with something soft and supple.

"Oomph!" his victim let out as they fell together to the ground.

Ephremael's wrist blade was out and pressed against his assailant's throat before he even had a chance to make sense of what had gone wrong. Huge frightened eyes stared back at him in the most striking shade of purple he had ever seen.

Of course, he thought, cursing his own incompetence. He had known that Lianzet was not alone. He was jerked out of his thoughts by a sharp stab under his ribcage and awoke to the realization that there was a sword threatening the flawlessness of his skin.

"Sneaky girl." He said with a sneer.

"You may remove your blade from my neck." She replied smugly.

"Why yes of course." He said, as though he had forgotten it was there, slowly choking the life out of her. *Just a beautiful doll,* he thought to himself. *She's God's puppet and nothing more…But what an exquisite puppet.* He found himself admiring the perfection of her smooth porcelain skin, her long slender neck elegant as a swan, and the faint rosy flush on her cheeks. *In another world,* he thought.

The sword lodged under his ribcage broke through the skin, causing him to wince and snapping him back to the situation at hand.

"If you would…" he gestured at the offending blade but she shook her glorious silver mane vehemently at him.

"You first."

He sighed, so he was going to have to do this the hard way.

"I hope you'll honor our agreement." He said; loathe to give her the upper hand.

"Unlike you, I still have a sense of honor." She hissed.

He smiled in spite of himself, amused by this fragile, fiery creature. He took his blade from her neck and with a flick of his wrist concealed it in his cuff. He felt the pressure on his ribs abate as Asielle relinquished her blade. He rolled off of her somewhat reluctantly and sprung nimbly to his feet, offering her a hand up. She refused with a look of distaste that for a second gave him a pang of regret, but that passed quickly enough.

"So," he said, smiling loosely, fingers ready to unleash his blades, "May I know the name of my opponent?"

She scowled at him as she rose from the ground with the grace of a falling blossom and he was struck anew by her impossible beauty, which she seemed oblivious to. She was lithe and willowy, all long limbs and perfect proportions, her cloud of silver hair floated around her like a halo and her brilliant eyes sparked with fury. *I can't help but approve of God's work on this one.*

"I see no reason for pleasantries. We are at war, you know."

"An unfortunate complication." He flashed her his most winning smile as he circled her slowly, her wary eyes fixed upon his every move.

"You know, we don't HAVE to be enemies, the I'rae could use a woman with your…qualities."

In response Asielle twirled her swords expertly, not even batting an eye as the sharp Uthicon-plated blades passed closely by her face.

"No? You would refuse my generous offer? I'd hate to scratch up that beautiful skin of yours."

"You won't be leaving here without a few scratches yourself." She growled.

"You disappoint me, but either way I will be leaving here with the Scrolls."

"Just you try it." She threatened as they both assumed battle stances, waiting for someone to make the first move.

Asielle

She was buying time, whoever this guy was he was surely a formidable foe. She could tell by the quiet mastery with which he wielded his weapons and by the practiced and lethal grace with which he moved. She doubted that she possessed the skills to win in this battle; he was the lion and she the lamb, helpless as he drew near for the kill.

She hummed softly to herself, desperate to add whatever strength she could, and the predictable glow of magic began to spread down her arm and into the blades. It tingled as it seeped through her veins lending her power that she alone had no hope of harnessing.

Her opponent eyed her with evident amusement; clearly he did not perceive her as a threat, which might act in her favor. She couldn't afford to lose, the stakes were too high.

His blade scratched her right arm, drawing blood as he sailed by her. She reacted with all the speed she could summon, raising her left blade to retaliate as her right blade blocked his. The jarring sound of metal against metal seemed to shake her soul loose from her physical body. Her left blade was caught in his, he sneered unpleasantly at her as she struggled to free it.

There was a rush of air and she felt his lips brush against her cheek and reddened visibly. He was taunting her, well aware of the fact that she was out-matched. *I can't rely on Lianzet to always be there to save me. I have to find the strength to protect myself.* Asielle's only real strength was her song, all Angels could sing, of course, it was practically a requirement, but no one could sing like Asielle.

Her voice was her own special brand of magic, unique in its power to invigorate the spirit and heal the most grievous of wounds. There were no words to her song, and somehow this made it all the more poignant. It was the sound of her soul laid bare and it struck a chord in all who heard it, awakening hidden places within them, or reviving long-dead, severed chords of their souls.

She sang now with her whole heart, the fierce blush coloring her cheeks the only acknowledgment that she was still aware of her enemy's presence. Her voice lilted and soared above and beyond the Heavens themselves. The air surged with the hum of magic and she could feel her cells filling with power. She reached out a hand towards the brazen I'rae and he was flung backwards by a burst of Holy power. It was more power than she'd ever summoned before and it was quickly mounting. She stopped singing, frightened of the unknown limits of her song. But something happened that had never happened before. The song continued on without her, the walls vibrated and the air began to sizzle. It echoed all around them, twisting her up inside.

Ephremael

Who was this girl? Ephremael reevaluated his assessment of the threat she posed. In the midst of their battle she had broken out into song, the strangest song he'd ever heard, the notes seeming almost physical in nature as they wrapped around his heart. He could still taste her, sweet upon his lips, and the sound of her ethereal voice warmed the blood in his veins and made that stolen kiss seem all the sweeter. He was enchanted by her, or was it by her song? There was something about her that stirred something slumbering deep within him. *She is what the heart dreams of while asleep.*

He had to stop this infernal song, it made him feel weak in the knees, a sensation he had never encountered before and which irked him terribly. He darted towards her, both wrists raised in slashing motion as he sliced at the air in front of her. His blades did not reach the target they sought, meeting with an invisible resistance which sent the strength of his strikes rushing back at him, nearly shattering the bones in his arms.

The girl shot him a terrified look and he realized she was no longer in control of her powers.

"This is not good." He murmured to himself, throwing a glance at the Scrolls. Now was the time to make a grab at them, she was preoccupied with keeping her powers in check.

Quicker than a snake lunging for its prey he made his move, but his hand hit living fire and he recoiled as magical flames leapt up his arm, threatening to singe his unseen wings. There was no pain in his reaction, but rather the memory of pain, a sensation no longer felt or perceived. *So, the Scrolls are magically protected.* He sighed, this was supposed to be a simple mission, but thus far there'd been nothing simple about it. Still he couldn't return empty-handed, and he had no intention of doing so.

He tested it again, more cautiously this time, letting his own magic flow through his arm to dissipate the flames. Though his magic did serve as a shield, slightly deadening the force of the force of the shock, it was clear he would not be able to break through the barrier alone. It would take a power far stronger than any mere Angel might possess, a far more ancient and primal magic, akin to the power that had created these abominations to begin with. He wasn't sure if there was any place left in the universe where such a power might still exist. Clearly completing this mission had become an impossibility.

The song twined its way around his mind, scrambling his thoughts into a less than coherent mish-mash. *Ah, yes, the girl,* he'd almost forgotten her existence, so wrapped up he had been in completing his task.

She was looking straight at him, all traces of fear vanished, and he got the unsettling feeling that something else was also seeing him through her eyes. Something not altogether right, something that no longer belonged to this world, which lived in a very different sense of the word. This girl held more secrets within her than anyone had the right to, and certainly more than he cared to know. It was best to leave this place behind while he still could, the hairs on the back of his neck were standing up, a sure sign that things here were about to take a nasty turn for the worst.

Asielle

She was levitating. Asielle found herself longing for the security of solid ground but she'd lost all control of her body now, a victim to her own song. She felt helpless as a marionette with its strings cut, never to move again by its own volition or be prompted to it by its master. Possessions sometimes occurred amongst the living, when more powerful souls than their own exerted control over their bodies but she had never heard of a single instance where such a thing had befallen an Angel or any other being of celestial origin. But she had no other explanation for it. Her limbs felt like they belonged to a stranger, even the air in her lungs felt alien to her, burning her like acid.

It was like one of her nightmares, only this time she was awake, feeling as out of body as a ghost watching themselves die. She wanted to scream out for help, longing desperately for Lianzet's quiet strength and worldly wisdom. Even the renegade Angel observing her coldly from afar began to look appealing. She moved her lips, struggling as though they were stuck together by sap but no sound came out. She tried again and this time a voice emerged, but it was not her own. It was strange on her tongue, this voice that was hers and yet not hers, like an exotic spice that she had yet to develop a taste for.

And the words it spoke, less words than noise, like the crackling of a dying fire, a language unlike anything she'd ever heard, almost visual, as though every sound conjured up an image, clear and tangible without aid of imagination. And what images! Sound and light and love in the absence of darkness, fire without flame and snow like ash, beings neither living nor deceased and a raw, red sun whose cruel heat she swore she could feel. What it all meant she couldn't hope to know.

Then the air around her cracked, literally cracked, falling in visible shards to clatter on the floor with a baleful moan. And the Seal shattered. She heard it breaking before she saw it, a sphere-shaped bubble of liquid light. There appeared a visible crack, at first just one but soon it spread branches, coating the bubble with spidery veins. Light escaped through the fine cracks and then the entire room was filled with it, blinding and not without physical force.

As though a vortex had suddenly been opened both Asielle and her enemy were sucked towards the broken Seal by gale-force winds that seemed to cause even the walls to wobble. For a reason she would never fully understand, the crimson beauty grabbed hold of her as they were drawn inexorably inwards, cradling her head against his broad chest as if to shield her. She had no time to protest, the Seal was pulling at them like a greedy black hole, hungry for their extinction. She and her unlikely companion dug in their heels with all their might, straining against the wind to no avail. Despite the hole in the floor worn from their combined effort, they were losing the struggle.

And then with a loud pop that would've caused lesser being's ears to bleed the wind vanished as quickly as it had appeared. Their bodies, now leaning against an invisible force, teetered precariously and then they collapsed in a heap on the floor.

The I'rae smiled at her, still maintaining his protective hold.

"This is the second time we've fallen like this, are you sure you're not doing it on purpose?" She could almost hear the wink in his voice.

She pushed at him, her anger sparking the air that hung between them. It wasn't enough that this oaf kept crushing the life out of her but now he had the gall to suggest she enjoyed it? It was no wonder he'd fallen from Heaven's grace.

His attention had already shifted, the realization that his goal was now within his grasp lit across his face. With horror Asielle deduced that the Seal had been the only thing keeping the Scrolls safe, and she had inadvertently made their theft possible by disabling it.

They both made a dash for the Scrolls, shoving against each other, his sharp elbow jamming into her ribcage with such force she imagined an inaudible snapping of bone. They reached them at the same time, each laying claim to a Scroll.

Ephremael

The Sacred Scroll was rejecting his touch, as if it somehow knew he was no longer on the side of God. Shudders of revulsion swept through him as electric jolts nipped at him incessantly. He eyed the second Scroll, clutched with firm resolve in the girl's hands. He didn't know if the Scrolls held any individual power, they might be nothing more than shreds of common hide if separated. Mystic objects always had the strangest of rules.

"Hand it over." He ordered, forgetting that fleeting compulsion he'd had to protect this Angel. He'd worry about that later, when there was time to worry about such things. Right now, she was reduced to nothing more than someone who had something he wanted, something that to his mind belonged to him.

"Never." She declared defiantly, raising her blade. She was down to only one now; the other had been lost in the earlier chaos and lay buried somewhere under the rubble that now filled the room.

"I'm done playing." He warned, his voice more menacing than he'd anticipated.

"So am I." she replied straight-faced.

"I admire your courage, but you know that you can't possibly win."

Her face betrayed no emotion as she answered coolly, "Even if I lose, I still won't let you win."

His blade nicked her shoulder, then her wrist, but she gritted her teeth and squeezed the Scroll tightly. *Foolish girl*, he thought as she parried his next attack only to have his second blade sink into her side, creating a deep gash. She winced; clearly she was still capable of feeling pain. The heart is what caused the body to feel pain, and the less connected one was to their heart, the less pain was registered. Ephremael had not felt pain in more than 12,000 years.

She lashed out wildly and her blade grazed his cheek, a lucky blow. He moved in quickly, burying his blade in the soft skin of her belly, his other hand on the small of her back, pushing her forwards into the blade. Silver blood oozed from the wound, saturating her light blue robe.

"Mmph…" a small whimper of pain escaped from her lips and he felt a surge of unwelcome emotion, was it guilt?

She fell against him unstably, every muscle in her body throbbing with shock as her blood pooled around her feet, a sparkling silver lake. Her hand fell limply against his chest and looking down at her face he could tell she was fast losing consciousness. He reminded himself that she was the enemy, that he would soon obtain that which he'd sought and victory would be his, but it seemed in the moment a hollow victory. He felt as though he had just broken something terribly precious like stolen innocence.

He wanted to get away from this girl and all the confusing emotions that came with her. It would be easy to snatch the Scroll and run yet he was hesitant. He had killed before, both men and Angels and never had he felt even a glimmer of remorse, but now all he could think was: *What have I done?* He withdrew his blade from her side, silver blood coating it to the hilt and found himself reaching out to stroke her cheek, pale now without the rosy blush of life. She was cold to the touch, she looked up at him through lowered lashes, and then her eyelids fluttered closed.

"Wait…" he said, flooded with uncertainty and the strange and unwanted sensation of having lost something. "I don't even know your name…" That seemed an inane thing to say. What did her name matter? What did she matter? Nothing but the Scrolls mattered, and yet they were the very last thing on his mind.

He cradled her lifeless body in his arms with the conviction that helping her was the only way to make this terrible gnawing sensation go away. Before he even had the chance to consider what that meant, something collided with his skull with a sickening splatter and enough force to cause him to drop to his knees.

It was the lifeless body of the imp, its head cleanly severed with frightening precision.

"Lianzet," he said, not bothering to turn his head.

"So…you know me, but I do not know you, foul scum of the Heavens."

Ephremael let the girl's body slide to the floor and stood to face Lianzet. The Angel's face was twisted into a mask of rage most fearful to behold. His eyes were piercing flames of hatred, his fury so potent as to be palpable.

Lianzet closed the distance between them with unimaginable speed, there was murder in his glare as he swung his scythe at Ephremael, who barely managed to block it with his blades. *His strength is incredible*, he marveled. Lianzet's skills were legendary and Ephremael had often fantasized about facing him in battle, naively optimistic of his chances. He realized now how foolish of a notion that was, his pride had convinced him he was the best, but there was no comparison here. His right blade broke under the weight of the scythe, its tip shaved off by the blow and a fracture running along the remainder. This was a fight he could not win.

Ephremael's eyes darted to the fallen Angel at his feet, the Scroll tucked securely in her fist. He leapt back from Lianzet and made a frantic grab for the Scroll but his foe was far quicker than he had any right to be and blocked his attempt with an ease that made Ephremael feel something quite like fear. He would have to cut his losses and run. Clearly, whoever this girl was, she meant something to Lianzet, enough to invoke the full force of his wrath.

"Heathen…I'll have your head for this!"

This time he didn't manage to dodge the blade completely, it caught in his left wing and the dreadful sound of shredding filled the too silent air. Lianzet was clever, without functioning wings Ephremael would be stranded and at his mercy.

"Tend to your companion." Ephremael said, beating his wings slowly as he rose into the air. "She will surely die without treatment."

His flight was lopsided, his left wing drooped at his side, lame and nearly useless, more hindrance than help. Lianzet's keen gaze darted between his fleeing enemy and his fallen friend. This slight pause was all Ephremael needed, with a flick of his wrist he opened a portal to the outside in the ceiling above him, and with one last longing glance at the beauteous Maiden of Heaven he shot through the portal leaving nothing but stray feathers behind him.

As he struggled through the flight home he was plagued by the image of her face, pale as moonbeams, her silver hair soaking in a halo of her own blood. He'd never killed a thing of such beauty and he felt a pang at the thought that he'd never encounter the fair creature again. *At least I got a Scroll*, he told himself, but a voice very much like a conscience nagged at him that it hadn't been worth the cost.

5 CHAPTER FIVE

Asielle awoke in a panic, her hand grasping with futility for the absent Scroll. Lianzet was slumped in the chair beside her, hands clasped over his face as though some great calamity had befallen him. Her blood still sang with the sound of battle, adrenaline causing her ears to throb along with her heartbeat. Was it over? Had they lost?

She remembered the searing pain, the I'rae's wicked smile as his blades shaved her life away. Then a wave of roaring blackness, that shut out all her senses until she was utterly alone in a way she'd never been before. There was a world of murky darkness, as if she was deep underwater in a place that only faint tendrils of light could reach. Nothing breathed here, the air so heavy it couldn't sustain life and she had the strong sense that she did not belong here. Was this the death of an Angel? This half-life obscured by a shadow world? How had she come here? And then came a crack in the darkness, a booming voice at once familiar and strange and she felt herself being lifted into the air by a warm, gentle breeze. She had felt the words in her core, pumping life back into her frozen veins. *Go,* the voice thundered. *Go my daughter.*

"God…" she whispered out loud and Lianzet's head snapped up as he threw both arms around her in a hug so fierce as to steal her breath.

"Asielle! Oh thank the Heavens! I thought that I'd lost you."

She bolted upright in bed, sudden dread seizing her.

"The Scrolls! Lianzet—" she didn't have to speak, the question was evident in her eyes.

Lianzet shook his head, "You managed to save one, you did well."

"The I'rae…he escaped?"

"Don't worry about that now, even Angels need to rest."

The door to the Healing swung open and Baukutet breezed in.

"Ah, look who's awake." She said with a gentle smile. She hovered over her, hands spread out as she read her aura.

"Well, there seems to be no permanent damage." She winked at Asielle playfully. The mild-mannered and cheerful Angel of Healing was one of Asielle's favorite people, second only to Lianzet in her heart. It was hard not to like her; she was always kind and benevolent with never a harsh word for anyone.

"Poor Lianzet here was absolutely distraught, why he was a complete wreck; he cares for you very much you know." Baukutet said with a 'tsk', her warm eyes like melted honey crinkled in a slightly disapproving smile. "I haven't seen such atrocious wounds since the last war...oh when was that?" she mused, then shrugged as he failed to remember, " Ah, well it was quite some time ago, anyways, and I'd much prefer not to see such injuries again, if you don't mind."

"Yes, I'm sorry...if only I were stronger the Scrolls would still be safe." She hung her head in shame, she had worried her friends for nothing, and she'd been unsuccessful in her duty.

"Now now," Baukutet chided, "There's no need for self-pity. I'm sure that you did all you could, the I'rae won't get their grubby little mitts on the second Scroll thanks to your valiant efforts."

"I should have been there. Those injuries...should have been mine to bear. I am so sorry to have failed you, Asielle." Lianzet's large frame was wracked with sorrow and guilt as he left the room.

"So dramatic, that one," Baukutet commented. "Well, you'd best go tend to his wounded pride, eh?"

"Thank you, Baukutet." Asielle said, rising out of bed, not a hair on her head out of place from her prolonged slumber.

"Asielle, wait a moment."

She turned to face Baukutet as she tossed a glittering object at her. She caught it deftly, the fine chain like wind-swept ice in her palm.

"What--?" she inquired.

"It's the scale of a Sea Dragon." She explained, tucking her long copper hair messily into a loose ponytail. "Their healing capabilities are quite legendary."

Asielle turned the large scale over in her hands, admiring the ocean of color within its reflective surface, as though a piece of the sky had fallen into the ocean and crystallized on the creature's back. The chain was spun from unicorn mane and glistened like white flame in the light.

"I cannot take this. Surely, it is precious to you."

"What need do I have of such a trinket, I haven't seen the battlefield in many centuries now. Take it, it will help augment your innate healing powers and aid in your recovery. Hopefully it will keep you out of my office, hmn?" she cocked an eyebrow at Asielle then chuckled, "Unless of course, it's a social call. I do so enjoy having company over for tea time."

She lifted the curtain of her hair out of the way as she put the necklace on, protectively covering the softly glowing pendant with her robe.

"I shall treasure it." Asiellle said sincerely, bowing her head in respect. Baukutet waved her hand in dismissal.

"Yes, yes, don't you have an Angel to catch? Off you go!" Asielle smiled gratefully at her and darted out the door into one of the hundreds of gardens that graced the Holy City.

"Lianzet! Wait up!" she called, using her wings to catch up to his long, hurried strides. He didn't stop walking and she grabbed at his arm to show him down. He whirled to face her and she shrank back, made timid by the anger evident in his expression.

"What were you thinking, Asielle? What possessed you to take on that fight alone? I thought you were aware enough of your limitations to not take such foolish risks!"

"Lianzet…" she recoiled as if shot, shocked by his coldness. "I only thought to protect the Scrolls."

"The Scrolls could have been retrieved, Asielle! Your life could not have been! Do you understand how close we came to losing you forever?"

"Y-yes I know I was careless. I apologize for that but I was only doing my duty."

He grabbed hold of her by both arms and shook her, forcing her to look directly into his blazing eyes where she saw a sort of quiet desperation she had never witnessed there before.

"Do you understand what losing you would do to me, Asielle? Do you not know that it would destroy me?" he looked earnestly at her as though searching for answers in those deep, violet pools.

"Destroy you…?" Asielle repeated, incredulous. What was he talking about? "Lianzet the Indestructible felled by little ole me?" she gave him a playful punch, attempting to lighten the mood and hoping for a smile to break across his face like the dawn after a storm.

He sighed dejectedly, the air rushing out of him like wind through a tunnel. He seemed exhausted and Asielle fancied that she could see deep hollows appearing under his eyes, though this was of course absurd.

"Yes, Asielle, you hold that power." He said wearily, "Just…just promise me you won't put me through that terror again." There was a silent plea in his eyes and she realized with a start just how serious he was.

"Lianzet…I-" she felt a selfish tear springing to life in the corner of her eye and she shook her head, wishing it away. "I'm…really sorry. I did not mean to worry you so." She didn't really understand where all these emotions were coming from; she had run after him expecting to comfort him with whispered reassurances, but this? This was not at all the kind of conduct she expected from Lianzet. She felt a sudden urge to distance herself from him, as though by staying she would somehow only make things worse.

"Um, I—I have to make my report," she stammered, whisking away, strangely eager to consult with Halliel, of all people.

Ephremael

"What is this?" Olucard asked, his lips curled in obvious displeasure.

Ephremael knelt on the obsidian floor before him, with its veins of gold glittering in the torchlight.

"My apologies, General, I was only able to recover one of the Sacred Scrolls. There were…unforeseen complications."

Olucard harrumphed as he lounged in red velvet throne he had acquisitioned for himself during the plundering of a castle.

"And just what am I suppose to do with only ONE of the Sacred Scrolls? Their words hold no power without their counterpart."

"Lianzet was there, milord."

Olucard clenched his jaw and gripped the arms of his throne with such ferocity that the wood began to splinter. Olucard despised Lianzet, his hatred for him far surpassing his hatred for Halliel. Olucard had considered Lianzet his rival for many millennia, and was gripped by a terrible rage whenever his name was mentioned.

"Lianzet-" he spat as if the very name itself were distasteful and somehow repugnant to his senses, "is nothing more than a bothersome thorn in my side."

"Be that as it may, I was not prepared to face him." He said, artfully leaving out the fact that he'd been woefully out-matched and would never stand much of a chance against Lianzet's prowess.

"No of course you weren't," Olucard replied dismissively, with an ease that rattled Ephremael's sense of pride. He rather unceremoniously flipped the Scroll open and peered at it intently. His brow furrowed until his eyes were reduced to slits of a menacing green.

"Ephremael, come here," he said lightly, in a tone that warned Ephremael that his brother was in a foul mood. Olucard had never been much for familial love and it showed in his treatment of his younger, less ambitious brother. As far as he was concerned, Ephremael was just another pawn in his quest for power and just as disposable as every other soldier in his army.

Ephremael approached tentatively, wary of Olucard's wrath and peered obligingly over his brother's shoulder at the unrolled Scroll.

It was blank, as naked as the night sky when stripped of its stars. His eyes widened in shock as he stared at the Scroll as if words might appear if he only looked harder. He had risked his immortal life for this? This piece of velum that held no more magic than a strand of his fine red hair?

"It's blank." He blurted, instantly regretting speaking.

"Blank?! Yes I know it's blank my dear brother, but WHY is it blank?!" Olucard roared, and for a brief second Ephremael feared he might rip the Scroll in half.

"As you said my lord, the Scrolls hold no power while apart," he posed it like a suggestion, trying to soothe his brother's rage.

"Useless!" Olucard ranted, flinging the Scroll to the icy floor and pacing in aggravation.

"The Angels must be encountering the same issue with their Scroll, at least that must be of some small comfort."

"That the Angels have managed to lay their hands on a Scroll at all is only due to YOUR extreme incompetence! Better to have left them as they were than to have even one fall into the hands of Angels!"

"It was they who broke the Seal and released the Scrolls. If I had not been there they would have them both." Ephremael retorted, beginning to lose his patience.

"Do not try to defend yourself." Olucard snarled nastily.

"Oh, you do have such a nasty temper, Olucard." Said a voice from the shadows as Anguilla slinked into the light and coiled herself around a less than willing Ephremael. With her midnight blue hair and tinted red eyes she was a frightening beauty, curvaceous and seductive with a taste for destruction.

"Anguilla, do you have something to report?"

"Hmn?" she entwined her arms around Ephremael and peered up at Olucard through heavily lowered lashes. "The city of Etol fell within the night, my liege. It was child's play. The King of Tyrin is much pleased with our services and my men are on their way to claim the promised relics."

"Mm, some good news at last. Perhaps I should've sent you in Ephremael's stead."

Olucard cared not for gold or jewels, for of what use were such baubles to Angels? What Olucard collected, or rather stock-piled, were mystic relics that could aid in his crusade against God. It was a steep price to pay for an Angel's favor, but the mortals paid it gladly, trading magic as if it were water. They traded for land, allegiance, conquest, murder, assassination and the promise of victory. Truly they were a race inspired by greed.

Ephremael shook Anguilla off as if she was a disease sucking away at his life. He had no appreciation for her dark brand of beauty.

"So, what of this Seal? Was it of the Bellavie? You know how such things fascinate me, Ephre."

She was a scholar of sorts, if you could call her morbid obsession with destroyed races that. Particularly of interest to her were the Originators, the Bellavie race, of which next to nothing was known other than the fact that they had existed before even God and had more than likely dwarfed his power. The Scrolls were thought to be their doing as undoubtedly was the Seal that had accompanied them.

"My name is Ephremael." He said, and though annoyed he obliged her request and described the Seal and how he'd been unable to disrupt it, which piqued Anguilla's interest.

"That Seal should've been out of the power of anyone but God to break. How then, did you come into possession of the Scroll?"

"The girl…"

"What girl?" Olucard demanded, frustrated by the entire conversation.

"Her song broke the barrier."

"A spell? What strange sort of magic is cast through song? Do you recall the words?" Anguilla inquired, infinitely curious.

It was something he failed to describe, a nonsensical event that seemed more fantasy than reality. Frankly he sounded insane, a song in a language comprised of images instead of words, two separate voices joined in one unknowing entity, an Angel with the power of a God? No matter how he attempted to describe it, it was outside of the capacity of words to convey. In the end he gave up, how could he explain something that even having witnessed he did not understand himself?

While Anguilla was only interested in the subtleties and details, Olucard latched on and held fast to the bigger picture. This girl was clearly a problem. Whoever she was, she held great magic, and the how didn't matter so much.

"If this girl truly possesses the power to break a Seal of that magnitude, then she is a threat to us all." Olucard declared.

A threat? Ephremael laughed. "The girl can barely fight. And I—"

"You what?"

"I doubt very much that she survived our encounter, she was grievously injured." He couldn't keep a note of regret from seeping into his voice and Olucard eyed him suspiciously.

Anguilla shrugged off his assumption, "Nothing with that much power can be so easily disposed of."

Could she have survived? Ephremael was hesitant to hope but the prospect caused his heart to sing.

"Hmph. The second Scroll is out of our reach for now. As much as I relish the thought of wresting it out from under Halliel's watchful guard. Anguilla, find out where it's being kept, and what they've been able to decipher from it. I must know if both Scrolls are blank or if my fool of a brother was tricked into stealing a decoy."

"Aw, but I just got here, me and Ephre haven't had our chance to catch up yet," she said, trailing her polished fingers against Ephremael's chest. His magic field nipped at her like a snake rudely awakened from a sun-drenched nap, and she giggled and spun away.

"Yes well, there is no one else I would entrust with this task," Olucard replied, cunningly appealing to her sense of pride. Anguilla took the bait.

"I suppose I am the only hope you've got. But do send sweet Ephre along with me or are you sending him off to bungle another mission?" she oozed a sweet, syrupy sickness that made Ephremael reel with nausea and before he realized he'd spoken he'd volunteered himself for a mission he found only slightly less revolting than Anguilla's company.

Asielle

Her wounds were gone, little more than scars on her memory, but still Asielle felt torn, pieces of herself scattered to the Universe, bleeding her soul dry. But why? What was this hollow through which life breezed without backwards glances? She had not felt herself since hearing that strange voice, singing that strange song that somehow seemed meant only for her. She didn't want to be any different than she already was but how long could she avoid the undeniable truth that no matter what she wanted she <u>was</u> different. Different in every way that mattered. Who was she? <u>What</u> was she? Was it something she could ever know? Whose voice had spoken through her, and whose soul now instilled in her the certainty that something was missing, missing in her. A void that she had never sensed before, that demanded to be filled, but with what?

Asielle tugged at her own hair, it was all too much for her to think about and her head was beginning to hurt almost as much as her heart did. Whatever it was she was longing for would have to come find her, because she had no clue where to go looking for it.

"Asielle, you needed to see me?" she looked up, completely taken by surprise by the utterance and very nearly collided with an aloof Halliel. She was even more shocked to see him forgoing his throne and emerging from the Judgment Chamber, without the dim light and intimidating atmosphere he looked like an entirely different being. She was forced to admit that he was quite radiant.

"Halliel, about the Scrolls I--"

He cut her off. "Lianzet already informed me of the events at Callion Library. What he failed to explain to me is why you were there in the first place, and how it is the Seal came to break."

"You knew about the Seal? And yet you sent Lianzet to retrieve the Scrolls knowing full well he'd be unable to?" she was livid, had the whole thing been a setup?

"Calm yourself, though I wouldn't mind seeing Lianzet fail for once, I wasn't certain that he would. I had only insubstantial reports on the Seal, though it seems it would have been out of his power to dispel. You are not known to possess great power, my little Asielle, so how is it you managed to break a spell only God himself should've been able to disrupt? Hmn?"

There was something different in the way he looked at her, a sort of cool calculation as if he were reappraising her worth. She wasn't sure how much to tell him, the truth was she had no idea how the Seal had broken, nor how much she'd had to do with it. She suspected that Halliel knew more than he was letting on, but how much more?

"Asielle…" his voice had softened, "Do try not to get yourself killed just yet. I still have need of you."

"…Really, Halliel? I very nearly died, and that's all the compassion you can muster?" She wasn't sure why she was so incensed, of course she couldn't expect any sympathy from Halliel, he was not known for compassion. *Even Angels are allowed to have bad days,* she told herself.

"Don't act like I don't care, Asielle. If you'd only stop being so stubborn, I'd gladly show you how much." He said, putting his arm around her.

Ick, she thought, squirming out of his embrace. His skin prickled like thorns on a cactus, clearly something she wasn't meant to be in contact with. She shouldn't have given him that opening.

"I've no time for your games, Halliel. I'm…I'm not well."

Halliel seemed momentarily confused. "Baukutet assured me you'd made a full recovery." He stated.

"I don't think it's something she can mend…"

"Explain." Halliel snapped, clearly irritated.

And it all came out in a rush, the flood-gates opened despite any reservations she held. When it was all out, lying there naked and prone to scrutiny she tried to read Halliel's blank expression, fully expecting him to laugh and proclaim her mad. Instead, he seemed to be taking her words quite seriously, mulling them over in his mind with intense deliberation.

"This is…a matter I must look into." He said finally, as though hesitant to let the words leave his mouth.

"You believe me?" she asked, surprised. Now he looked at her as though she were crazy.

"You are many things, Asielle, but a liar has never been one of them. It is against your very nature. Now, it is surely a strange tale, and I know not what to make of it, but perhaps God's guidance resides in you."

Now <u>that</u> was crazy.

"In me?! Don't be absurd!" she protested.

"How else do you explain it, Asielle? Clearly you were lent Higher

Powers, and I know of no one else able to conjure the powers of the Bellavie."

She started to tell him that she thought she'd heard God's long-absent voice but thought better of it. Surely that voice had been the construct of her exhausted mind and its desire for comfort.

"Sing for me." He commanded abruptly.

"Wh-what?" she asked, suddenly bashful.

"Sing for me." He repeated. "Let us see if it was a one-time occurrence or not."

Asielle was no good at singing under pressure, pressure in battle was entirely different than being put on the spot by one of her peers and she balked, wanting to dismiss the entire event and move on. Halliel was insistent however and eventually she relented and sang for him. Her voice was lovely, as it always was, and it drew all the hovering Angels to it like moths to a flame and an appreciative crowd began to gather around them. Asielle squeezed her eyes shut tight in a sincere effort to pretend they weren't there. Though beauteous and evocative, it was her voice alone that came forth, no mysterious undertones and no outside force borrowing her body. She was admittedly relieved; she never wanted to feel that helpless ever again. The siren notes still hung in the air as the song came to an end and the crowd slowly dissipated, reminded of urgent errands by Halliel's lowered brow.

"Well, that was certainly magical." He said, and she detected a twinge of disappointment in his voice. "But the only voice I heard was yours, Asielle."

He regarded her thoughtfully. "Perhaps if I were to endanger your life..." she searched his face for a hint of playfulness but he was all seriousness.

"Asielle, the Scroll you retrieved, are you certain it's one of the Sacred Scrolls?" he asked almost conversationally.

"Yes of course, it never left my possession."

"Hmn," was the only response she received.

"Why, Halliel? Did something happen to it?" she was struck with a sudden fear that perhaps the Scroll hadn't made it home with her after all.

"It seems to be blank." He said simply.

"Blank...?" It was like a cruel joke, she'd come close to the surrender of her immortal life for a blank Scroll?

"I suppose it is only in God's power to read," he said. "Or perhaps it is spelled. Either way, we must decipher it before the I'rae make sense of the Scroll in their possession."

"May I...can I see it?" she asked.

Halliel shrugged and took the Scroll out from under his golden cloak. Asielle took it with trembling fingers, unrolling it slowly, her eyes prepared for stark white, and at first that's all there was. Then, as she stared, words began to form in her mind, and then transcribed themselves onto the soft, worn velum. She glanced at Halliel surreptitiously but he made no sign of seeing what she saw. The Scroll was clearly not blank; it was covered in words any Seraphim could read. Why then was she the only one who could perceive them? Her life had been fairly stable for centuries, every day much like the last without any major deviations but suddenly there was nothing familiar and everything unknown. She had never before been so confused about her own existence and she missed the safety of the familiar. Would she ever feel that again, or was this turmoil permanent?

She rolled the Scroll up carefully and handed it back to Halliel without saying a word. She didn't want to know what it said, didn't want to be singled out. It was best for everyone if the Scrolls could not be read; only Gods could be entrusted with that kind of power.

"Asielle, no missions for now, I don't want you leaving the safety of the city. And I don't want you near Lianzet, he almost got you killed." He said it as if it were just like any other order he might issue, instead of what it really was, a personal vendetta.

"You can't really expect me to avoid my closest friend. You have no control over me, Halliel, you are not God."

This made him angry, Asielle wasn't normally so bold and he did not appreciate being challenged. He pinned her arms to her sides and growled at her through clenched teeth.

"Let me be very clear, Asielle, I have never pretended to be God, but I am in charge in his absence, and you WILL obey me, do you understand?"

She struggled against him but he was tremendously strong and his grip was unrelenting no matter how she squirmed.

"Halliel, let me go."

"Stay away from Lianzet." He repeated.

"You can't ask me to do that."

"Your friendship with him places your life in jeopardy. I'm merely concerned for your safety."

She scoffed at that, "My safety? If you cared at all for my safety you wouldn't send me on such dangerous missions! You've been trying to get me killed for centuries, and now that you very nearly succeeded you're blaming Lianzet?"

His face blanched, "I did not send you on that mission. Lianzet was not authorized to bring you along."

"I did not know he needed your permission," she replied snarkily.

"Do you really think I want you dead, Asielle? I know you'll come around to my way of thinking eventually, and I have all the time in the world to wait for you to do so." He seemed appalled at her accusation.

"I'd rather be dead…" she whispered dryly.

His fingers dug into the delicate skin of her inner wrist like claws, causing her to cry out in pain.

"You should really watch what you say, darling…" he snapped, his breath hot and unpleasant on her face.

She couldn't run fast enough, her feet inadequate to the force of her fear. She didn't think to fly, she didn't think at all, all logic overtaken by the simple primeval desire to flee. The very grass seemed to hamper her escape, slender blades licking at her toes, cool green tendrils of seduction lulling her into a false sense of safety. She fought against its fallacious reassurance, feet so light she floated like a weary cloud pregnant with rain towards her destination.

The doors to the Healing flung open in obedience to her frantic kinetic energy and she relaxed slightly at the sight of its familiar rosy walls.

"Mm? Back so soon, are we?" Baukutet poked her head up from behind a pile of haphazardly stacked books, her hair mussed from reading.

"I wouldn't think you've had time enough to get injured again."

"No, it's not that. I—" Asielle sunk down against the wall as it pulsed with warmth, easing her tensed muscles and slowing her rapid breath. Pulling up her knees she rested her chin against them, cradling them against her chest in an attempt to comfort herself.

"I know not what brought me here. I do not mean to intrude."

Baukutet rose and made her way over, sinking gracefully to the floor besides Asielle, copper hair pooling out behind her, released from the constraints of its ponytail.

"There are no intrusions amongst friends. Now, what is it that troubles you?"

Could she say? How much could she unburden on such a benign soul? How much about the Scrolls, about herself, could she reveal? Her harried mind could not formulate the answers, thoughts fretful and incohesive. When her lips finally mustered a sound, it was only one word.

"Ha…Halliel."

"Ach, I should have known. What has that ruffian done now?" Baukutet scanned Asielle's cowered form, skillfully honing in on her hands clasped protectively over her injured wrist, silver veins glimmering with agitation through luminescent skin. She removed Asielle's hand gently, taking it in her own as she tenderly surveyed the wound with the lightest touch of her fingers.

"That man, he may be able to lead the armies of Heaven, but he lacks any semblance of social graces. And you, my dear, have the vast misfortune of bringing out the very worst in him."

"He's nothing but a brutish boor." Asielle spat, feeling petulant as a spanked child.

Baukutet laughed cheerfully as she tended to the wound, redirecting the wayward blood back into the veins where it belonged.

"You make it too easy for him to provoke you." She commented gently. "Your reactions only fuel him, running away will only further incense him anger."

She knew Baukutet was right, but how could she hope to react in any other fashion?

"You speak as though I shouldn't resist him…"

"Oh, no, you must resist him. He is not worthy of you, Asielle."

"Try telling <u>him</u> that." She glowered.

"You know," Baukutet spoke tactfully, as she comfortingly stroked Asielle's tangled hair, frizzed out with static like the fur of a belligerent cat. "The closer you become to Lianzet, the more Halliel will seek to pursue you."

Asielle was immediately up in arms.

"So I should punish Lianzet for Halliel's transgressions?"

"Ah but you are fiery, child. The more you fight back the more you'll entice him. Halliel is a conqueror; it's what he was born to do. Make yourself less of a challenge and he may lose interest. It is no fun to conquer those who don't fight back. Besides, you know how Lianzet dotes on you, if Halliel were to win over your affections, he would have bested Lianzet in the most important arena of them all. A victory neither of them would soon forget."

"So I am to be relegated to the position of a trophy? To the winner go the spoils, and I am such spoils?" Queasiness was fast overtaking her, and she fairly spat out the venomous words lest they burn a hole through her tongue.

"Hush now, surely Lianzet does not think so, but Halliel is…a baser sort. I do not suggest that it is an easy position, simply that you attempt to douse the flames rather than fanning them."

Asielle heaved a sigh at the complexity of it all, such subtly nuanced behavior was quite beyond her and questioning her every reaction sounded both foolhardy and tedious. And yet, her current pattern of behavior had not served her well, so perhaps there was some worth in Baukutet's sermon after all.

There was the unmistakable clatter of paneled wood as the forceful timbre of Halliel's voice made contact with its selectively yielding nature. Though he had the respect and decency not to force his way into this quiet sanctum, he had no qualms in bellowing until the walls made way for him.

Asielle wanted desperately to pretend that she hadn't felt the rumble through her feet, nor witnessed the crystal floor sprout fine spider silk cracks in response to the jarring sound. She wanted to stay hunkered in the soothing warmth exuded by Baukutet, to be a coward without needing excuse, but Baukutet was not encouraging of denial. She pulled Asielle to her feet with her and gently set her to right.

"Now, you know that you may stay here for as long as you wish, but the longer you tarry, the more unreasonable in his fury he will become. It would be easiest for you to confront him now, before this escalates further."

Asielle hung her head in admission of the veracity of this statement, and quietly squeezed Baukutet's tender hands in gratitude. She knew that thanks were never needed here, but felt compelled to offer them nonetheless.

"Thank you, Baukutet, as always you have provided me with aid when I am most in need of it. My appreciation." She dipped her head slightly in deference to the older, wiser Angel, and slipped out the door before her resolve to face the storm outside crumbled just as the walls threatened to do.

When Asielle emerged from the warm, ensconced safety of the Healing she was stricken by an emotional chill, brought upon her by the nearly visible waves of resentment radiating off Halliel. He was clearly incensed by being forced to temporarily abdicate his throne and stray from his place of power. *He did not have to follow*, she thought bitterly.

Under the weight of his stare Baukutet's words seemed feeble and naively idealistic. When had running away become such a theme in her life? Had she been forever harboring a coward, only now to realize it? To parry with anger, to cower in fear, would only further antagonize this madness. She knew, and yet every fiber of her scattered being longed to react just so. And what was it in her that met confrontation with such infantile animosity?

She spoke demurely with hands clasped together, with the thought to diffuse Halliel's rapidly burning fuse.

"I apologize for running from you, Halliel. I should not have done so."

He was not receptive to her pliancy, if anything he was staunchly resistant, seeming to take it for an insult he encroached upon her personal space as aggressively as ever before.

"Nobody…" he hissed, his breath intoxicatingly hot upon her face, "runs from me Asielle. Not even my worst enemies have the gall to flee when faced with my impending wrath. Your insubordination can no longer be tolerated!"

"When have you ever met me with even a hint of tolerance, Halliel? My very existence seems to be intolerable to you!" His roiling frustration was infectious, and she found herself taking the bait yet again.

Halliel loomed over her, the coldness of his shadow washing over her and causing her skin to prickle with apprehension.

"Your constant ineptitude and defiance of my authority should have been dealt with long ago, though I had not the heart to do it! My favoritism of you blinded me to your many faults and transgressions, but your childish willfulness will be quashed here and now. You will obey me, Asielle!" He reached for her, and her hands strayed to her swords.

"Like hell I will!" she proclaimed angrily, all the while wondering whether she really intended to draw her blades against the self-proclaimed leader of Heaven.

He snatched up her wrists and heavy-handedly wrested them from her sides, twisting her hands backwards roughly so that she was forced to relinquish her grip upon her blades, which clattered uselessly to the ground at her feet.

"Ah!" she kicked out at him and he twisted her arms violently, his fingers leaving harsh red marks upon the pale tenderness of her skin.

"I will have no more of your foolishness, Asielle. You shall not defy me." She winced as he tugged her viciously towards him and she fearfully wondered what he might intend for her. She wrenched her lower body away from him and froze him with her glare.

"You shall not tame me, Halliel. You may have everyone else here following your every whim, but my will is no less strong than yours, and the only will I shall submit to is Gods!"

Halliel's eyes sparked with such ferocity that Asielle half-expected them to catch fire. She knew questioning his authority was not the wise course of action, but she could hardly think straight when confronted with such pervasive hostility.

"You WILL submit, Asielle. My will is the will of God, and what God wills is for you to submit yourself to me!" He started dragging her towards him, her heels digging into the dirt as she struggled against his might.

"No! Let go of me!" she yelled as she futilely attempted to reclaim her swords with her feet.

"Let her go." Lianzet's voice was a low, guttural growl, fraught with menace.

"This is none of your concern, Lianzet." Halliel retorted, shooting him a venomous glare.

Asielle felt warm liquid anger flow through her veins and stab at her skin. She was sick of this, sick of being stuck in the middle, of having to always be protected, of being weak. No more.

"Both of you, just leave me ALONE!" she pushed at Halliel, hard as she could. He barely even blinked. Frustrated, she thought back to the immeasurable power that had raced through her only days earlier and though it terrified her, the thought of being powerless was still more frightening. *Please,* she thought, *help me.*

Lianzet seemed shocked by her outburst, or perhaps hurt. "Asielle..." he said softly.

"I just—I just want to be alone for awhile..." she felt her old weakness welling up within her, threatening her eyes with tears and she bit down on her lip to stifle them. Halliel would just keep pushing his limits unless she put her foot down. She could see it in his eyes even now, his eagerness to kiss her right there in front of Lianzet, or maybe even because of Lianzet.

"Halliel…" she said slowly, building up to it.

"Yes, my sweet?" he replied, though there was nothing affectionate about his tone.

"Let…me…GO!" she squeezed her eyes tight and shoved him with all her might, imagining waves of electricity humming through her system and a raw, uncontrollable power pulsing through every cell.

When she opened her eyes Lianzet's face was frozen in horror and Halliel was crumpled on the ground several feet away in a sizzling, smoking crater. *It worked,* she thought with surprise. She had only half expected it to work without the song but her silent plea had been answered. It was even stronger than before and she had a sudden vision of this forbidden magic incubating inside of her, growing stronger and stronger until her frail body could no longer contain it. What would happen if she couldn't tame it? She had only meant to force Halliel to release her; she hadn't wanted to hurt him, though now she worried that some small part of her might have desired just that.

Overwhelmed and frightened of herself, the only person that she could truly trust, she let her guard down and the tears came, fast and plenty. She grabbed her fallen blades and took off before anyone could notice, flapping her sparkling wings as rapidly as she could, wanting nothing more than to be far, far away from here. She didn't care that Lianzet would fret or that Halliel would be furious, or even that she might be banned from Itsukuenel, the only home she had ever known, for the assault. None of that seemed to matter anymore, her head was swimming and the whole world seemed upside down. Without a specific destination in mind she flew blindly through the still blue skies, with a sense of urgency she had never felt before. So absorbed in her own thoughts was she that she honestly didn't hear the desperate bellow of Lianzet's voice as it ricocheted off the walls of heaven.

6 CHAPTER SIX

Ephremael

Ephremael followed behind the sobbing girl, more intrigued than he had
been before after the events he'd just witnessed. It had definitely been this
girl who had broken the Seal for him, her Holy power was undeniably
strong and it was equally clear that she had not fully harnessed it yet. He
would have to tread carefully, it now seemed she could summon her powers
at will and he had no desire to be on the receiving end.

That handsome blonde Angel she'd had an altercation with must
be Halliel. He'd been relieved and strangely thrilled to see him go flying
across the gardens, even silently cheering. He'd been oddly upset by
Halliel's hands all over the alluring Angel. It shouldn't have provoked him,
of course, but he had the slight, nagging sensation that if she hadn't handled
it herself he might have been compelled to interfere. He'd never felt
protective of anyone in his millennia of existence, it was a brand new and
peculiarly pleasing feeling. He wasn't sure what it was about this girl but
there was clearly something special about her and he didn't seem to be the
only one who noticed. The two most powerful Angels in Heaven were
fighting over her; he chuckled with amusement at that. She was certainly
fascinating, this breath-taking and fragile creature.

His wings cut silently through the cloudless skies for quite a while,
feeling a small pang each time a tear plummeted to earth, wondering with
idle curiosity where they might fall. Though his wing had healed completely,
the long flight began to tire him and he hoped they would soon be landing.

As if she had heard him, she began to drift slowly down through
the air to a mist-coated island that he did not recognize. Staying concealed
behind thick cloud cover he matched her movements with expert stealth.
She touched lightly upon the ground with a natural grace not even the most

skilled of dancers could hope to master. It was a field glorious with flowers that glowed and shimmered like starlight in an array of iridescent blues and purple and pale white leaves like moonlight. The tree line loomed in the distance, tall with firs and evergreens and warm water in bejeweled hues broke in creamy waves along the coastline.

He ducked behind the only object in the field large enough to hide his tall frame, a large weathered boulder of honey-colored brown. She fell to her knees amidst the flowers, held her head in her hands and sobbed until there were no more tears left in her. Then she just sat there, entwined in stony silence as the hours slowly ticked by and Ephremael began to fidget with boredom. The light started to trickle away, gobbled up by the encroaching darkness as a tropical breeze blew through the enchanted field.

Finally, just when Ephremael could bear it no longer, she stood and faced the rock he hid behind. *She can't possibly see me*, he thought nervously, crouching down just in case.

"I give to you my song; I lend to you my voice. May you use it to create many blessings and in return bless me with strength of spirit." She proclaimed to the empty air. Confused, Ephremael sought the recipient of her words but the only breaths to stir the island air belonged to him and her. It took him a while to realize that the speech was directed at the second presence within her, whose existence he had previously only guessed at.

"Who are you? Where are you? Please…answer me." She pleaded, much like a desperate mortal begging for their prayers to be answered. Of course, there was no answer, just a deafening silence broken only by the soft susurrus of the wind. The Angel sighed as if defeated and then clasped her hands tightly together and began to sway delicately as the notes of her melody filled the air. As she sang, her hair fanned out like a halo around her, glowing like the moon that was slowly rising in the sky. The flowers near her waved and bowed before her as if pledging their allegiance. From within her a pale golden light began to emanate, separate from any other source. The air surrounding her distorted, crackling with invisible energy, and faintly, ever so faintly, a second voice joined in the song.

This voice was mournful, full of howling grief for something irreversibly lost. So potent was its magic that had he been able, Ephremael would most certainly have cried. Behind the singing Angel, a ghostly figure began to shimmer into being, wrapping its transparent arms around her. It was a woman of surpassing beauty, though to his mind she posed no comparison to the silver-haired maiden. She bore on her arms strange writings, as though her entire body was a scroll and she the living proof of its words.

O filia, the words were not audible and yet he clearly heard them in his head, and from the way the Angel stiffened he knew that she heard them too. *Quamdiu sunt quaerunt, quamdiu venti adempta animae praebet.*

"You've been searching…for me? If you know of me, then I've been searching for you as well. Tell me, am I Angel…or?" she had no words for the possibility of what she might be.

Ephremael listened for the answer with curiosity almost as keen as hers. Angels were not brought into being by traditional means and so had no mothers. Who then, was this phantom with fondness etched into every crease of her face?

What you are is for you to decide.

This was not the answer she had wanted.

"If you cannot tell me who I am, than at least tell me who you are." She said with evident exasperation.

I am nothing more than what once was and can no more be.

A riddle, Ephremael despised riddles, strongly preferring direct, straight-forward communication. This woman, or faded image of what once was a woman, was extremely irritating to him. The way she twisted her words like invasive ivy slowly squeezing the life out of an unsuspecting tree made the temperamental I'rae want to twist his hands around her insubstantial throat.

"That's not an answer!" the Angel protested, her eyes violent sparks of frustration.

It is all the answer that I have came the apologetic reply. *What I was once, I am not now, and as you were born is not as you will die. I am no more than a wisp against time, and you the dream that I carried in life.*

"So you're…a ghost then?" her tone was hopeful, specters were a concept she could understand.

I never lived as you lived. I was born of song and died of silence. There is no one now living that would recognize my soul.

"But you're…my mother?" she queried, searching for a straight answer. A gust of wind caused the apparition to quiver like a shudder through the air.

In as much as anyone could be. But it is not your origins that are of import it is the future you create with them. You are all that remains of me, don't let me be forgotten.

She started to fade away, the glow of the flowers shining through her transparent form.

"How can I forget you when I can't even remember you?" she was desperate, even more confused than before as she attempted to grab hold of the corporeal form and drag it into existence with her own insistence that it should live.

You will remember what is necessary to remember, and forget what it is necessary to forget. The voice was faint, distant as an echo fast fading into the night.

"Please, don't leave me! Tell me who I am!"

All your answers lie within; my song…is the only guidance I can give you…

And then she was gone, as transient as a breath on a cold day, though the Angel clung to her fading form, every note of her frenzied song full of a pleading despondency. Its quiet eyes and sad smile vanished last, filled with promised fondness and a longing for an eternally severed connection. Her translucent lips moved slowly as if weighed down, but were not graced with words or sound; an empty soul full of empty words.

The Angel stared after her long after all traces of the vaporous presence had dissipated. Ephremael expected her to cry, alert to the slumping of shoulders and the choked sobs, but none came. Just silence, endless silence, not even the hoot of an owl to displace the stillness. Her eyes mirrored the calm, but turmoil lurked just beneath the surface, threatening to explode violently into existence. He subconsciously took a careful step backwards, imagining he could discern clearly-defined forks of lightening waging war in the purple skies of her eyes.

The electricity running up her arms and frizzing up her perfect hair was not imaginary however, and its sharp crackle filled the air. Her pale bird-like hands were clenched tight in fists as unrelenting waves of anger caused her body to undulate. Tremors of rage made sparks of light flare off her luminescent wings. She was a sight both glorious and terrifying to behold and Ephremael couldn't seem to take his eyes off her. Otherworldly fire sprang to life around her, the flames greedily licking at her slender legs as tendrils of blue smoke grew on her like moss.

"All I ask," Her voice was trembling with her concentrated efforts to maintain control, "is to know who I am. Is that not the right of all creatures? Who am I? Who?"

I would like to know that as well. It was no longer about his orders, if indeed it ever had been. Ephremael genuinely wanted to know who this girl, this Angel who plagued his every waking thought was. The Scrolls weren't the only magical creations with counterparts. It was said that for every Star born, its equal was born in a distant place. This is how the Universe upheld balance, for every soul there existed a second soul, its reflection, its shadow, made up of all that the first soul lacked so that only together could they be considered complete.

Ephremael had never thought much of this theory, but now he began to wonder if perhaps it could be true, and if such a match existed for all species, then why not for Angels? Perhaps this seemingly unending fascination with this magnificent creature was something completely out of his control, and if this was so there was surely no need for guilt.

As he pondered this, the Angel wrestled with her frustration and the magicked flames spread across the field consuming the sweet night air, burning the stars with its heat though the earth remained unscorched. A strand of flame snaked its way over to the rock Ephremael sheltered behind, and with a resounding crack flailed against it like a whip. The boulder creaked open as a massive crack appeared and the rough stone was engulfed in suffocating flame. Ephremael moved stealthily backwards, one with the shadows, selfishly hiding his radiance from the light.

"Someone…tell me! Tell me who I AM!" with this last outburst the entire sky seemed to be lit by sparks and the blue fire of the netherworld leapt forth to claim the Heavens.

This is not Holy magic, the I'rae thought, slightly concerned with what he might have gotten himself into.

Disguised in the flames, faces were emerging, creatures he couldn't quite identify, vicious and fearsome. A dragon of blue flame loomed in the sky, dwarfing the moonlit Angel who seemed oblivious to the chaos she had summoned. Its coils wrapped around her protectively as its behemoth horned head turned with a deafening roar towards Ephremael, as though it could see him with its non-eyes.

"WHO AM I?" the Angel screamed and a massive shockwave spread from where she stood across the island. The trees bent and snapped, the flowers flattened, the fire beasts shrieked in terror as they were torn apart and spread to the wind. The rock imploded, scattering fragments into the turbulent sea and sending an unprepared Ephremael sailing through the flame-filled sky to skid to a stop just inches from cliff's edge. Digging his blades into the hard-packed soil he beat his wings against the puissant wind as his feet struggled for frantic purchase. A tree clattered past him into the sea, the force of its landing sending the sea to nip at Ephremael's ankles like an angry dog. With a grimace he hung on, battling for his continued existence until finally the forceful winds abated and he leaned wearily against his battered blades with a sigh of relief.

His respite was short-lived however. The Angel had been made aware of his presence and was staring across the field at him, her pupils so swollen that barely any white could be seen.

He braced himself for impact.

Asielle

At first it was just a glimmer at the edge of her perception, there and then gone again as her mind struggled to make sense of it.

The once lovely field lay in tattered ruin around her, tufts of the magic flowers floating through the air, resplendent reminders of their now lost glory. The sky blistered with the taint of numinous flame and a crater had formed in the ground around her, sucking life down into its voracious maw.

In a dream-like haze she observed her surroundings, her mind weeping at the trees ripped from the ground and tossed carelessly aside like so much refuse. She picked up a lifeless flower; it lay limp in her hand, a frail, broken thing. The purposelessness of this destruction pulled at her heartstrings and then a shaking dread overcame her, pushing against the corners of her mind and clamoring for recognition. Like a fleeting shadow it swept over her until she was covered in shivering darkness.

She had done this.

This unutterable obliteration that went against her most innate nature, was the product of her own grief. How could she, even in the grip of such dreadful anger, have wished for this? She hugged herself in an attempt to assuage her guilt and the wracking sadness that had so suddenly come across her in the wake of her unremembered fury.

And that's when she saw him; an unclear, yet familiar figure on the far side of the plain, struggling to right himself with a grace that attested to him as being one of her kind. In an odd way she was relieved to see him, another living creature in this vast expanse of death.

She glissaded smoothly over to him, landing delicately in front of him, closer than she should have been. He was more magnetically handsome than she had remembered and she thought he looked almost sheepish to have been caught. She regarded him with an almost vacant sense of curiosity, ignoring the nagging sense that she should be steeling herself for battle.

"Hello." He said conversationally, as though they weren't two beings balanced on opposing sides of a cataclysmic battle. His voice was rich and dark, soothing in a way that felt almost sinful. She felt uneasy under the full weight of his stare and shifted uncomfortably.

He cocked his head at her expectantly, his lustrous hair falling against his perfectly chiseled jaw, and she realized she'd been so caught up with silent admiration that she had yet to reply. A blush crept up on her cheeks and she fervently hoped that he hadn't noticed.

"You. Why are you here?" she asked, "Are you following me?"

He smiled with muted confidence.

"I'm not looking for a fight."

"No? Then what are you looking for?"

He shrugged nonchalantly. "Well, I should think it would be obvious, I was looking for you."

The blush was spreading along the full curve of her cheek, heating her face in a slow, pleasant rush.

"You've found me."

"So I have." It was obvious that he hadn't been prepared for a confrontation and she could almost hear his thoughts racing to arrange themselves. She wondered how she would fare if it came down to a fight, but a groaning in her soul warned her that she'd had her fill of destruction for the day.

"We've met before, at Callion." He said.

"I remember. How could I forget the fiend who nearly stole my life from me?" she countered, a hardness creeping into her voice.

He took a cautionary step back.

"I am truly sorry about that. I am much relieved at your survival." He offered her an apologetic smile that certainly seemed genuine.

"So, if you have not come to finish the job, what have you come for?" she asked, refusing to be distracted by the perfection of his smile.

He faltered, searching for an acceptable answer and finally settled on the truth.

"I came out of curiosity," he admitted. "I want to know who you are."

She laughed bitterly. "As would I."

"Your name would do for now." He prompted with that bedazzling smile.

She tried to gauge how serious he was; realizing the most dangerous thing about this I'rae was his undeniable charm.

"I'm…Asielle." She answered guardedly.

"Asielle…" he repeated, savoring the sound on his tongue in a way that made her squirm.

"A lovely name." he beamed at her and took a step towards her, hand held out cordially. "If we're going to keep running into each other like this, we might as well exchange names, don't you agree, Asielle?"

The tone with which he said her name sent a shiver down her spine, a sensation which she was ashamed to admit was not entirely unpleasant. How strange this was, to be standing here in isolation enjoying a casual conversation with a sworn enemy. She had thought of the I'rae as brutal beings on the verge of becoming daemons, but this man with his wings that shone like the sun, he seemed just like her. How could anything this beautiful be evil?

"I'm Ephremael." He said, extending his hand further, his smile never wavering.

It didn't seem to be a trick. Keeping her eyes focused on his face, every nerve alive to incongruencies, she slowly reached out to shake his hand. As her fingers lightly grazed his, a jolt went through her, filling her blood with slow, delightful warmth. His long, slender fingers clasped effortlessly about hers, his large hand covering her small one. She felt her heartbeat racing in her chest and a faint sort of song resonating in her ear. It was like a dream overtaking her; she had never before felt such a sense of rightness. And it frightened her, terrified her even, how could she begin to make sense of this feeling? What could it possibly mean?

"It's very nice to meet you, Asielle." He said in a soft purr and she yanked away from him, startled.

"H-how can you say that?" she stuttered, "You cannot be friends with your enemies!"

He let out an exasperated 'tch' and lowered his hand back to his side.

"And yet, I find myself wanting to be your friend, Asielle. Is that so very wrong?"

She stared, incredulous; who was this man who thought the rules of warfare didn't apply to him? There was a subtle loneliness written on his face that mirrored her own, a loneliness that she did not care to acknowledge. She felt sorry for him, this creature whose pure, unadulterated sensuality made her breath stick in her throat. This sad, lonely beauty whose very beauty made his eternal loneliness inexorable; without something of substance to anchor him to this life, would he simply float away to be forever lost to the void?

He was watching her with unabashed fascination, seemingly memorizing every nuance of her face and she felt very self-conscious. She had never been very aware of her looks, she was an Angel and a certain amount of beauty was guaranteed, but she had never had anyone behold her with such avid concentration before and she began to wonder what it was he saw, and if it was pleasing to him. She found herself uncharacteristically longing for the simplicity that came with solving problems with violence. Drawing her trusty blades and hacking away was certainly less confusing than…whatever this was.

He laughed and her eyes widened at the unexpected sound.

"You look as though you want to hurt me." His voice was teasing, the implication was: you can't possibly hurt me. She scowled, resentful of the reminder of how poorly she had fared in their last encounter.

She should have just left, fled back to the safety of the Holy City, not engaged with the enemy in casual discourse any further, but curiosity won her over.

"Just how long have you been following me?"

It was the I'rae's turn to fidget, and she imagined she saw the barest hint of redness quavering upon his cheek and felt a smug sense of satisfaction.

"Long enough." He answered brusquely and she envied him for regaining his composure so promptly.

Should she have been outraged? Livid at his unwelcome invasiveness? Probably, but as unpleasant as it was, he had squirmed his way into a secret confidence with her by being the only witness to recent events. She couldn't bring up that strange, woeful ghost who spoke in riddles with Lianzet, it sounded too much like a fevered dream. But this gloriously infuriating man had been there for all of it and there was some comfort to be had in the knowledge that she hadn't just imagined it all.

"So you saw her, didn't you?" he seemed taken aback by the hopeful twang in her voice.

"I saw her."

She folded herself onto a fallen tree that hadn't quite managed to make it over the edge of the cliff, relief soothing away the tension in her muscles. Ephremael tried to gauge her reaction as he very hesitatingly edged forward and perched long-legged on the tree, close enough that their wings brushed, sending a shower of sparks to fall to the ground like stardust.

"You saw her…I was worried that I'd gone mad." She confessed.

Angels giving way to madness was not completely unheard of, though it had only occurred twice in all the epochs of their being.

"But if you saw her too, then she must be real…right?"

"Who was she?"

"I wish I knew." She hung her head forlornly so that her hair hid her from view like muslin curtains, shielding her from his relentless stare.

His wings stiffened with trepidation and stealing a peek at him through the gossamer veil she saw that he held his lower lip firmly in his teeth as he nervously contemplated something. She focused on her hands, suddenly very aware of his nearness, remembering the tingling sensation of his hand touching hers and the bewildering warmth she had felt in her heart, as if all along this had been what she was longing for, only she hadn't known it. She pictured Lianzet's face, how it would turn purple with rage if he were to espy her sitting in such companionable silence with a member of the opposition and grimaced with a deeply felt sense of compunction. Still, she was loathe to leave.

A faint stirring of motion, a gentle rush of air as fingers gingerly reached for her, entangling themselves in her silver tresses. Heat rushed to her ears, turning them beet red as Ephremael tenderly swept her hair from her face and tucked it with care behind her flushed ears. He chuckled lightly as he saw them, which only made them flare up more, so deeply red that they almost matched his hair.

"There," he said, smooth and sweet, "That's much better."

She felt as though she'd swallowed her tongue.

"Wh-what are you doing?!" she was frozen in place, her body longing to stay put while her mind screamed at her to get away. *Danger! Danger!* It warned, but still she stayed.

"I apologize, that was very forward of me, I only wanted to see your gorgeous face." There wasn't the slightest allusion of apology in his tone.

Gorgeous, he thinks I'm gorgeous? She felt panicked. She didn't know what she was meant to do in this situation, had never foreseen such a thing happening to her in her lifetime. Not counting that time with Halliel, she had never kissed a man, never wanted to share that intimacy with anyone before, never dared even think on it. These were brand new sensations for her, and she wished Lianzet was there to provide guidance, to explain these emotions to her in a non-frightening way that she could understand. And why was this situation arising only now, with an enemy of all people, someone she shouldn't even be speaking with? Was this something God had planned? Some cosmic joke at her expense? But then love was something out of even God's control.

She laughed at herself. Love, love was something not meant for Angels. She wasn't sure it was a feeling they were even capable of, she had love for Lianzet certainly, and Halliel had feelings towards her, but neither were a romantic love. Just because her heart throbbed and ached at the softness in Ephremael's eyes did not mean it was love. She didn't even know him, or how far from the light he'd fallen.

"How did you break the Seal?" he asked abruptly.

Oh, she'd been a fool. Here she was thinking he might actually like her, when all he was doing was probing for information. Of course, he'd been sent to spy on her, what did she expect? She had let her guard down and spun a fanciful story around his actions, drawing conclusions that were based less on fact than on her own hidden desires. She'd let him make a fool of her, swooning over his sugary words and melting under his blistering gaze.

She felt daft and thoroughly shamed.

She stood up hastily, obdurate with anger and humiliation. He rose with her, seemingly bewildered by her sudden change in behavior.

"Do you really think it wise to have come alone? You know what power I hold." She was bluffing and she could tell he knew it by the careless ease of his stance. He had no intention of fleeing.

"Your powers are incredibly inconsistent." He said, stepping sinuously towards her even as she backed away, it was like they were engaged in some bizarre dance. "I have faith that you won't use them against me."

Another step.

"How long have you had these powers, Asielle?" his eyes seemed to pierce through her very soul, prying her open in his search for the truth.

How long? She considered it, had she ever heard that mysterious voice before that day at the library? Had it always been within her, lying in wait? Was it only her utter desperation that had called it forth from deep inside, or had it been some outside force? She searched her mind earnestly but kept returning to the same conclusion. *Callion, Callion, Callion.*

"The library, that was the first time, wasn't it?" he asked as though reading her mind, and she struggled to adopt a blank expression. "You'd never been so close to Bellavie relics before." He mused aloud.

"I have nothing to do with the Bellavie." She protested.

"You may not know it, but you clearly do." He seemed enthralled by the prospect. "That woman…could she have been one of them?"

If Angels and demigods were mythic beings amongst Mortals than the Bellavie were their equivalent amongst Angels. There was ample evidence of their existence, but no clarity about the details of their lives. Asielle thought back to the woman's murky visage, she had not looked so very different from an Angel, though she lacked their ephemeral glow and their majestic wings. Her eyes had been sunk deeper into her skull, so dark the iris was indistinguishable from the pupil. There had been faint symbols drawn upon her forehead and along the tapered bridge of her nose, tattoos?

"Asielle, do you know where you come from?" he pressed, his words crawling under her skin and festering there like open wounds. She wished he would stop saying her name.

"Of course I do." She sputtered.

"Do you really?" his tone was dripping silk as he took another flowing step towards her. She retreated, her heel caught against a slab of rock and to her absolute mortification, she tripped.

He caught her in one effortless motion before she could even attempt to right herself, his palm braced against her lower back and his free hand clasping hers against his brawny chest. He favored her with a self-satisfied smile that fueled her embarrassment.

"Careful there." He whispered breathily, leaning in so closely that his soft lips caressed the top of her delicate ear. She pushed back, her heart accelerating at such a pace that she gasped for breath.

"I-I'm fine, you can release me." Her eyes were wide and wild like a deer confronted by a hunter.

His eyes were innocent as he replied: "Now, why would I want to do that?"

For the space of a heartbeat they stood there staring at one another, turquoise into violet, light into dark, neither knowing what to do, both afraid to break the silence, and perhaps it was not meant to be broken.

"This is only the second time we've met," he said slowly, "and yet it feels as though I have known you always. Always…wanted to know you."

She gulped, her mind devoid of suitable responses, just numb with shock that she couldn't explain. This was not at all like her earlier confrontation with Halliel, when his hands had felt so alien and wrong upon her body that she'd wanted to peel her skin off and flee. This felt comforting and safe, and how could she possibly feel safe in the arms of the enemy. *In the arms of the enemy*, her thoughts echoed, was that really where she now found herself? He certainly didn't feel like an enemy to her, even though he had tried to kill her last time. Tried to kill her…

She lurched away from him.

"You tried to kill me! How can I keep forgetting what you are? You're I'rae! And I'm of Heaven and always will be! We are destined to kill each other!" her voice didn't come out as strongly as she'd hoped for, seeming small and timid in the vast expanse of the island, her words easily swallowed by the ravenous wind. Her wings loomed behind her, poised in preparation of flight.

"I won't ever kill you, Asielle. I can't." It sounded like a promise on his lips, but how could she believe anything he said?

"You stabbed me," she pointed out, "multiple times."

He looked ashamed and his pitch dropped so low that she had to lean in to hear his words.

"I am not proud of that. But as you said, it is war. As soon as I looked into your eyes, I knew I'd made a mistake. God, you confound me, Asielle, you fascinate me so. I can hardly draw a breath without thinking upon you. Have you spelled me with your song?"

She realized then that he was just as befuddled by all this as she was, though her mind could not move past his usage of God's name, which seemed against every code of honor that she knew. He almost seemed hopeful that it was magic that drew him to her and she wondered fleetingly if she should confirm his suspicion. For all she knew of her newfound powers that may very well be within her capabilities, though a little chord in her heart protested most vehemently that it wasn't.

"If it was a spell, I hereby release you from it." She proclaimed, waiting for a cloud of sudden hatred for all that she was to chase the blue from his eyes, but there was no change in his expression. She pretended not to notice the tiny flame of relief that ate away at her heart.

"Not a spell then," he sounded wearily disappointed.

She started to apologize then caught herself, what did she have to apologize for?

"Ephremael," she said, the name foreign on her tongue. His face brightened at hearing his name roll off her lips. "You really must let me go."

He glanced down at his arm which was still wrapped tightly around her back, tucked under the curve of her radiant wings, caught off-guard by her statement. He hesitated, and not sure if he intended to release her or not, she decided to make it clear it was less of a suggestion and more of an imperative.

"All I have to do is start to sing, and I can force you to let go." She presaged.

This turned out to be the perfectly wrong thing to say. A slow, deliciously evil notion tugged at the corners of Ephremael's mouth, drawing his lips into a scarily seductive smile. He drew her in close against him though she flapped her wings in futile resistance.

"See, the thing about that is…you need your mouth." He smirked.

Her expression was blank, what an obvious thing to say, of course she needed her mouth to sing.

As his hand cradled her head firmly from behind and pulled her towards him, recognition slowly dawned upon her face and strangled apprehension sank in.

He meant to kiss her.

She gazed upon his face, now only inches from hers and even more magnificent in proximity. If she wanted to wrest free of his embrace she had best do it now, for it was fast becoming too late. Her muscles refused to obey her commands, and she felt as though her body was leaning willingly into the anticipated kiss, melting into his warmth like snow. Did she want him to kiss her? She couldn't make up her mind.

So someone made it up for her.

Just as Ephremael's sensual lips came close enough to her own that she could feel the static charge between them, a voice boomed out into the silence with a force that could split mountains.

"STEP AWAY FROM HER!"

Lianzet had found them.

7 CHAPTER SEVEN

Asielle's scream tore through the air as Lianzet's scythe sliced through the meager space between them, effectively forcing them apart. His face was set in a grimace of such immense hatred that even the night breeze seemed to flee from his path.

Damn it, Ephremael thought as his fingers were pried apart from Asielle's. How did he find us?

Lianzet was upon him like a rabid dog, claiming his scythe from where it had torn the ground asunder and swinging it at him with berserk ferocity. He clearly meant to kill him. Ephremael dodged the onslaught with easy dexterity and leapt to the sky, eager to survive the encounter. With a whoosh that rattled his heart against his ribcage with excruciating might, he hit the ground, the force of the impact creating a crater. Lianzet had grabbed hold of his wing and hurled him from the sky. With a vicious wrenching motion he snapped the wing in his hand and loomed over a broken Ephremael, who howled with the embittered pain of one who had forgotten what pain felt like.

"Stop it! Lianzet!" her shriek was plaintive and paralyzed the blood in Ephremael's veins.

The bronzed Angel towered over Ephremael's prone form, his large foot stomping down on his ribs with a nauseating crack. A gargantuan fist crashed into Ephremael's well-defined cheekbones, grinding them into dust and sending sprays of blood sizzling into the cold night air.

Asielle lunged for Lianzet's arm and pounded furiously on it but he seemed unaware of her presence so blinding was his wrath. Mercilessly he struck at Ephremael, turning his flesh to pulp under his rapidly pounding fist. He was brutal and relentless as a war God and there was no hope of blocking his attacks. The I'rae curled up into a ball, attempting to shield his head from the flurry of blows as he used all of his magic to divert as much force as possible. His eyes were swelling shut in his battered face and darkness was encroaching upon his vision. As he tried to fight it off he saw Lianzet raise his scythe up to deliver the killing blow, eyes hardened with steely determination.

"No! Stop!" Asielle launched herself in front of Ephremael, arms spread wide in a defensive stance and her eyes fixed beseechingly on her friend.

Drifting in and out of consciousness, Ephremael wondered just what their relationship was to invoke such unholy ire in Lianzet. He was far more terrified of the Angel warrior than he had ever been of Olucard or even of God.

The scythe continued in its downwards motion and Ephremael forced himself up on his elbows as the urgent need to protect Asielle filled him with a reserve of strength. She squeezed her eyes shut and winced in preparation but the pain never came. The scythe lingered inches from her face and then clattered to the ground as all the fierceness vanished from Lianzet's face to be replaced with astonished horror as he realized what he'd almost done.

She's…safe, Ephremael thought, finally giving into his exhaustion and fading away to a place where not even pain could hope to reach him.

Asielle

She waited for the sting of the scythe as it carved through her flesh like butter but the whistling of the blade through the wind ceased and an uncomfortable silence settled in. She strained her eyes open one at a time, not wanting to see Lianzet's kind, handsome face warped into that hideous mask of anger. He had been an almost unrecognizable monster and it had taken all her will to not shrink from him in terror. What demon had possessed him to set upon the unarmed I'rae with such vengeance in his heart?

His eyes were hollowed out by sorrow as he relinquished his fevered grip on the scythe.

"Asielle…" he choked out, slumping to one knee, "Why?"

Why? It was becoming the question that defined her life. Why, and who? There were so many 'whys' and not enough answers to accompany them. Why did she possess these strange powers? Why had that apparition appeared before her? Why was she the only Angel who suffered from the uncertainty of not knowing who or even what she was? But she knew without asking which 'why' it was that he sought answers for. Why him?

The unutterable pain in her friend's eyes was unbearable. There was a haunting sense of tortured betrayal that made her heart quaver with doubt as though a hole had been ripped open in her heart that would never again be closed. What could she say to staunch this ache, to banish the inexplicable agony from Lianzet's golden eyes? She floundered for the words to save her from drowning in this ocean of remorse but her mouth was dry and her mind numb.

Lianzet's face was drawn and tired and he looked shaken by some ancient sadness. She had wounded him mortally; she could tell by the way he shirked from her touch as she tried to ease the concentrated tension from his furrowed brow. Her heart broke at the intense hurt she perceived in his aura, and though she wasn't sure exactly what she'd done, she knew it had been unforgivable. She hadn't kissed Ephremael, but maybe it didn't matter if she had or not, she'd consorted with the enemy, and that was enough to earn her friend's distrust.

She had never seen Lianzet so afflicted; he seemed almost human in his uncharacteristic state of weakness. All the anger had vanished from him, leaving him defeated and small as a chastened child. She wanted more than anything to comfort him, to enfold him in her arms and soothe him as his large frame was wracked with sobs. To pretend none of this had ever happened and take his hand and go home, but was she still welcome there? She moved from Lianzet's side, turning her back on him so he wouldn't see all the emotions flickering across her face like reflections across a still lake. She had been the cause of his suffering; she had no right to cry and she was very aware of that.

"Lianzet, I—there's really nothing that I can say." Her voice was catching in her throat and tears trembled in her eyes waiting for their turn to fall. "I only hope that…you can forgive me."

The urge to escape rose in her again, that increasingly familiar longing to avoid complications and return to simplicity. She knelt by Ephremael's prone form, he still lived and would recover. It was a relief, but as long as he survived there would always be the threat of another encounter looming over her, who knows what might happen next time? It wasn't something she could afford to think about right now. When he regained consciousness he would seek her out again, she knew that with every fiber of her being. Sooner or later she would be confronted again with those nameless feelings of passion and pining and there was no way she could prepare herself for that. She wasn't sure she could maintain any control when around him, or even if it was worth trying to resist him. She looked at those lips, parted in remembered anguish that had come so very close to kissing hers and wondered what it would have felt like. Had she missed out on something amazing? She shook herself, what was wrong with her? These weren't normal thoughts, normal notions, her encounter with this I'rae was turning her entire world into a place that she had never seen before and herself into someone she no longer recognized.

Lianzet was watching her closely, he had risen to his feet and his body was rigid at her proximity to his conquered foe. His eyes dripped with a promise of menace, wary of signs of life. She stepped away, not wanting to create any more trouble, and glanced at her friend, uncertain of what was to come. He held out a hand to her, voice stern as he said:

"Come."

"How can I go with you, after what I've done?" her voice was a tiny whisper on the wind. How could she face Halliel? Where did an Angel belong if not in Heaven? Where did she belong? Did such a place exist?

"I've caused you so much trouble…I'm so sorry." She couldn't look at him, couldn't stomach her only friend's immeasurable anger.

He could sense her inclination to flit away, the nervousness of a trapped bird as it rattles against its cage.

"Asielle, stop."

Her wings flapped of their own accord in their agitated need to fly and escape the judgment in Lianzet's eyes. He reached for her in the same instant her feet left the ground, holding onto her arm like an anchor. It wasn't only symbolic, Lianzet had always been her anchor, and her link to the life she had thought was meant for her, part of the identity that she had built for herself. She had always felt like she belonged as long as Lianzet was there besides her, comforting her with his unshakeable strength. Raised as she was in the air, Lianzet was forced to look up at her, his eyes firm and pleading. Though he didn't say it, she felt a wordless communication from him: Your place is with me.

Is it still? She thought, was it ever really? Had she ever belonged in the Holy City, could she belong again?

"I came to bring you home, Asielle." His voice reverberated through her blood, stilling the tumultuous waves of her heart. "I am not leaving without you."

She broke down in tears, throwing her arms around his broad neck and sobbing into his ebony locks, breathing in the comfort he offered. His body softened as forgiveness awoke in his heart. He wrapped his arms around his fragile comrade and lifted them both up into the starry night sky for the long flight home. Her tears beaded into jewels in his hair, mimicking the night and glistening with soft beauty. His arms were tight around her, pressing her close and she felt suddenly drowsy and safe as a baby bird nestled underneath its watchful mother. Whatever happened, she couldn't lose Lianzet, and if his grip on her was any indication, he had no intention of ever letting her go either. Fears ameliorated, she drifted off to sleep as the moon sailed by.

8 CHAPTER EIGHT

Ephremael

When he awoke he was alone, more alone than he'd ever been before, more alone than he could ever be again. For one glorious moment he had tasted an intimacy with another soul that he had never dreamt possible, he had felt born anew in that moment, and died again in its absence. It wasn't something that he fully understood but he knew that Asielle had been the one to awaken this new life in him, and he craved the sensation again.

Asielle, what have you done to me? He wondered. He had no explanation for his recent behavior, other than some strange demon seemed to take hold of him while in her presence and his only desire became to be closer to her. It was an overwhelming and all-consuming compulsion whose only cure lay in satiating it. She had seemed to feel it too, her heartbeat rapidly accelerating as his skin lingered against hers, her ivory skin flushed and her eyes huge with expectancy. This certainly complicated things. If it came down to a fight between them, he was all too aware of his incapacity to cause any harm to the enthralling Angel, and what kind of soldier was incapable of wounding his enemy? She had a distinct advantage if in the heat of battle she was to turn those bewitching eyes upon him, how could he do aught but come to her aid, even against his own kind? His own kind…Olucard would not spare her life so easily and as insane as it seemed Ephremael knew that he would choose her life over that of his brother.

The thought made a sickness rise in him, she was a liability, and her very existence created a frightening weakness in him that greatly impaired his efficacy and rendered him nearly inutile. There was no way he could avoid seeing her, he knew enough about the ways of the universe to know that they would be inexplicably drawn together time and again. He was resigned to this inevitability, but he knew with an unrelenting certainty that he must keep Olucard from her. His brother had callously destroyed everything of import in Ephremael's life up till now, but he would sooner perish than to allow such a fate to befall Asielle.

His wounds stung like venom in his veins as he sluggishly staggered to his feet and tested his broken wing gingerly. His lips twitched with the effort and he gritted his teeth against the pain. Clumps of rain-hardened dirt clumped in the open sores, saturated with silver blood. He looked like the only survivor of a fearsome battle, as though he'd taken on the entire Army of the Heavens instead of one lone Angel. How weak Asielle must think him, so soundly and brutally defeated, crawling in the dust for his life like a worthless, pitiful mortal. This notion pained him far more than his corporeal wounds. This was the second time Lianzet had bested him in a fight and the admission filled him with shame. If Asielle had not been present he surely would have been killed, yet ironically it was her very presence that had fueled Lianzet's immense umbrage. It seemed he had a rival for her heart, when he wasn't even sure he wanted to be a suitor yet. If being a suitor meant holding the fair-haired beauty close against his heart and feeling life bequeathed through her kiss, then he supposed that was what he wanted. It was all very perplexing. These kinds of dilemmas were beneath Angels; at least that's how he had thought of it. Humans waged war over women all the time, but for Angels such a skirmish felt sordid and inexcusable.

He turned his sights towards home wearily and somewhat resentfully. His report to Olucard would be a difficult one to make and he was filled with dread. In order to protect Asielle he would have to lie about her involvement, and lying to his brother was an act of betrayal that would cost him his life if the discrepancies in his story were to be discovered. Ephremael had never risked his life for anyone but himself before and was loathe to do so now. But if he disclosed all that he knew of Asielle to Olucard, it would invoke a curiosity in his brother that could only end in bloodshed. Olucard eliminated any perceived threat with resolute and brutal haste, no matter what, or who, that threat may be. He had warned Ephremael many, many times in his life that he would not hesitate to dispose of him the instant he became a hindrance to his goals. He wouldn't even bat an eye over slaying the lovely Asielle, death meant nothing to him and he caused it with the impunity that not caring earned him.

Ephremael took his battered body to the sky as he pondered the complex turn his life had taken, wincing with the strain of each beleaguered flap of his disheveled wings. *Asielle,* his brain murmured her name over and over incessantly as if his heart knew no other words. He wanted her, that much he was sure of. Wanted her with a passion he had long thought dead in him. He had never thought of himself as an incomplete being, but each second spent by her side had alluded to a yawning emptiness pullulating inside his soul, a void that only she could fill. *She will make me whole.* He had to have her; there was simply no other way to quell this yearning that had arisen within him. Somehow he knew that he would find the answers in her smile. Though the world conspired to keep them apart he would win her for his own. *I promise you, Asielle, no matter what it takes, you will be mine.*

Assured of his eventual success he soared through the night, his glowing wings leaving an imprint upon the Heavens as coldness seeped into his veins, chasing out the warmth Asielle's touch had lent him.

Lianzet

Anger prowled through Lianzet's blood like a tiger through the night, frustrated by failing to locate the prey it sought. Asielle slept still in his arms and he relished the feeling, knowing that there existed nothing that could make this moment last. That cretin would surely come for her again; he had seen it in the I'rae's eyes, that maddening desire to be with the one who set your heart adrift. The way he'd had his hands upon her, as if his feelings gave him some claim to her filled him with a volatile craving for retribution. Death was the only thing that would keep the I'rae from Asielle; he knew that with sinking dread. If killing him was the only way to guarantee that Asielle would never again be put in such a compromising position, then he would gladly add another death to his eternally blood-soaked hands.

He glanced down at the slumbering Angel, her tear-streaked cheeks lighting up her face like trails of stardust. In her innocence and purity, she was more Angel than he would ever be; and he was determined to keep it that way. She stirred in her sleep and her hands became entangled in his hair. The mask of anguish he had worn on his face since the encounter with Ephremael began to lighten; she had not meant to hurt him with her actions. The pearl turrets of home appeared in the distance, hugged by the surrounding clouds. Rainbows arched over the city, setting it aglow in colored light. Somewhere beneath the veil of many hued clouds Halliel waited to confront their return. He would not find Lianzet easily cowed. He'd already had one man today attempt to steal Asielle from him; he would not stand for a second. He wrapped his strong fingers through her slender ones and squeezed gently, startling her awake. She glanced up at him through eyes luminescent as fireflies despite being blurred by sleep, and filled with more questions than he had answers for.

"Asielle," he said tenderly as a mother rousing her child. "We're home."

Asielle

Halliel was waiting for them, as she knew he would be, bitter resentment tattooed across his face. If she hadn't been safely ensconced in Lianzet's brawny arms she might have trembled under the weight of his glare that seemed to bore holes through her body. Lianzet set them down as softly as a feather floats to ground, not even ruffling the dust underfoot.

"Take her from here." Halliel spat, "Itsukuenel is no longer her home."

Asielle felt faint and her eyes stung with the pain of tears that weren't there. It was just as she'd feared, but the fear had been nothing compared to the dismay she now felt at the prospect of losing her home.

"Itsukuenel is the home to all Angels." Lianzet replied with a frigidity that made Halliel wary.

"You saw what she did to me, she is no Angel."

"You would do best not to turn your allies into foes, Halliel." Lianzet snarled, a warning too unequivocal for Halliel to disregard.

"No, it's…it's alright Lianzet. He's right, I don't belong here, I never did." Asielle said, hopping gracefully from Lianzet's arms. "I'll go, just please…don't fight."

"Asielle, don't listen to him. You have just as much right to be here as he does." Lianzet protested.

"That may be so but, he is right to fear me." She gestured at the destroyed garden. "Look at the devastation I have wrought, without even meaning to. Everywhere I've gone lately, all that follows in my wake is ruin. How then can you welcome me here? I'm…dangerous, Lianzet. I'm not like you…not like the other Angels, can't you see that?"

He shook his head. "It makes no difference to me, Asielle. You are not your powers; you control them, not the other way around."

She wasn't convinced this was true; somehow it didn't seem quite that simple.

"She admitted it herself, Lianzet, she puts us all in danger if she stays here." Halliel interjected smugly. His words were like daggers in her back though she tried her best to not let it show.

Lianzet's voice was deadly, his eyes molten slivers in his handsome countenance. "I am done taking orders from you, Halliel. With God as my witness, I shall not let you drive Asielle from this place."

"God?" Halliel echoed, his voice like a cackle. "What good is a witness that can't be found?" There was a calculating malice in his eyes as he fixed them upon Asielle's wobbling stare.

"Hand her over to me. The High Council will decide upon a fitting punishment for her crime."

The High Council was comprised entirely of Halliel's lackeys, there was no justice to be found there and that was a fact well known amongst the Angels. Asielle wondered if there could possibly be a penalty worse than banishment. Halliel was judge, jury and executioner of the High Council, but even execution seemed preferable to wandering the world alone and forgotten for the rest of eternity.

"This is obscene. She has done nothing to deserve punishment. We can easily repair the damage she caused in refusing your advances. I will not let you crucify her because of wounded pride."

Halliel's eyes narrowed into pinpricks of vehemence, his stance aggressive and anger born in every pore. "Lianzet, I grow weary of your insubordination, do not forget whose army you fight for."

"I have not forgotten. I fight for God, it is his will I follow and always shall." Lianzet retorted evenly, his wings stiff as sails.

"My army," Halliel corrected. "Do not be so foolish as to challenge that."

"You are not equal to me in battle." Halliel did not like to have his prowess challenged and his fingers lingered on the hilt of his greatsword.

"You may be a doughty warrior, but you cannot stand against the might of an army." His voice was laced with threats and Asielle feared for her friend. Lianzet was nothing if not loyal and she knew without a doubt that he would defend her honor to the death. She had to put a stop to this.

She wedged herself in between the two irate males, arms raised in protest.

"Please stop this," she pleaded.

"Step aside, Asielle." Lianzet grumbled.

"How sweet, she's trying to protect you." Halliel sneered, almost demon-like.

"No more fighting. Lianzet, I could not bear to see you get hurt. Don't make a foe of Halliel on my account, please."

"He made a foe of me the instant he made one of you."

Her heart sank at his misguided nobility, how could she hope to spare him from harm?

"Asielle," Halliel coaxed, "Stand before the Council, and this feud between me and your dear friend Lianzet will be forgotten."

"He lies, Asielle." Lianzet cautioned.

"That I know. But…what else can I do? I cannot let you fight my battles for me, Lianzet. I cannot lose you, you are all I have."

She'd never voiced that truth before, though the words came easy to her now. It seemed imperative, at this crossroads in time that he be aware of his crucial importance in her life. If he was shocked by her outburst it didn't register upon his face and his voice never wavered.

"Come to me Asielle, you know he cannot harm me." He held out an inviting hand to her, his eyes still fixed on Halliel.

"Lianzet, I-I don't know what to do." She closed her eyes and tried to think. How had she gotten herself into this situation? She could think of no action to take that wouldn't further muddle the situation. Surrender seemed easiest, but Lianzet would surely fight for her freedom and a Heaven divided was the last thing she wanted. She surmised that an apology wasn't enough to mend the circumstance either, and a display of her unreliable powers would only add fuel to Halliel's argument. Her mind was a tangled web of possibilities that all seemed to end badly, with every turn in thought a dead-end. Her senses were dimmed to her surroundings as she fumbled her way further into a quandary.

She didn't hear Lianzet's warning shout until it was too late and Halliel's keen blade cut into her throat. He pinned her arms tight against her back, exerting more force than was necessary, a cruel grin flashing across his eyes when she yelped in pain.

"Halliel!" Lianzet thundered, "You've gone too far! Release her at once!" he took a step forwards as if to enforce his order and Halliel's blade bit further into her flesh, slowly leaking blood.

"Stay where you are, Lianzet." Halliel growled, pleased to see him so helpless. "If you provoke me, my blade might slip."

Lianzet's teeth were gritted together as his voice hissed out from between his clenched jaw.

"Halliel, for every drop of her blood that you spill, I'll take a hundred of yours."

"If you hadn't been so stubborn, I wouldn't have had to spill any at all." Halliel jeered as the blood trickled to the ground. "Her pain is your doing."

Lianzet reeled back as if he had been struck, the thought of bringing harm to his friend cut him more deeply than any blade might.

"Don't hurt her." It sounded more like a plea than a proclamation and Halliel smiled at the knowledge of his victory.

"Hurt her? Now what a waste that would be." He lowered his blade and pushed Asielle roughly in front of him. "You will await your sentencing in the detention chambers." He said, shoving her forward, arms still pinned.

"And, Lianzet…" he shot back over his shoulder, "Don't interfere, lest you wish to cause her even more pain." He yanked on her wrists and she let out a strangled whimper. Any sign of rebelliousness faded from Lianzet's face at the sound and he stood there crest-fallen as Halliel dragged her off towards the dungeons.

The dungeons were as dreadful as the rest of Itsukuenel was beautiful, it almost seemed as though they descended into a different, more darkly lit world. The dungeons were a relatively new addition, when the heavenly world had been at peace there had been no need of such a place, just as there had not really been a need for the Healing and Baukutet's specific skill-set. The I'rae were very seldom taken alive, but when they were they were brought here to await trial and eventual execution.

As Halliel prodded her along down the spiral staircase, Asielle's thoughts grew increasingly darker the further they traveled from the light, as if the shadows on the walls were crawling into her mind. She could hear the walls bemoaning the fates of those who had traversed these stairs before her and she wondered if it was not only the I'rae who had fallen from God. Every century that this war dragged on the Angels became less like angels and more like the humans they were meant to watch over. Was it not a human trait to persecute and to hate thine enemies? What place did a dungeon, a source of nothing but great suffering, have in the Holy City?

They reached a cell, dank and obsidian black and reeking of unspoken fear. Claw-marks raked across the sheer stone walls and forsaken feathers lay strewn about the floor. Three slats of slender light was all the illumination available, an unnatural light for the sun's rays did not reach this far below ground. Halliel pushed her ahead of him, crushing her wings against the back wall. She pretended not to feel as his fingers slowly caressed her face in a gesture that was almost tender.

"What have you made me do, Asielle?" his tone was surprisingly remorseful and he heaved a laden sigh. "You've put me in quite the predicament. This cannot end well for any of us."

She knew that he did not expect an answer and so she offered none, sinking slowly to the floor to bask in the tiny pool of light as Halliel closed the heavy door behind him with a clang that stirred in her bones.

"This cell has an anti-magic shield," he said, "But I wonder how it would fare against someone with your talents."

It was an invitation, a kindness she had not expected from him. She matched eyes with him and understood. If she ran, she would never again be welcome here, and for the rest of her life Halliel would hunt her down as mercilessly as any I'rae. It wasn't worth the risk, though she could tell that Halliel wanted her to take the easy way out, he must have known that she wouldn't.

He stepped away from the door and she listened to the sound of his footsteps receding to leave her alone in the unfamiliar darkness. She wanted to sing to herself, wanting the comfort of a living presence to eat away at the emptiness which lay thick and foreboding in the air but her fear of the unknown robbed her of even that small modicum of consolation. What if she were to sing and inadvertently free herself? Then there would be no hope of acquittal, no hope of returning to the world above. She hugged her knees tightly to her chest and rocked silently back and forth as time slowly trickled away from her and the day passed into oblivion.

9 CHAPTER NINE

Ephremael

He'd been kept waiting long enough, and Ephremael had never been known for his patience, but then again he'd never come across anything worth waiting for. An audience with his infuriating elder brother definitely didn't make the cut. He knew that his brother was not earnestly engaged in important meetings beyond that heavy, sound-engulfing mahogany door. It was simply a demonstration of power, reminding his brother that he could leave him waiting outside eternally if it so pleased him. Ephremael was in no mood for such games today, and so he unceremoniously flung the doors open and strode uninvited into the inner sanctum where his brother regarded him appraisingly.

"I don't recall summoning you." He said snidely.

"I've come to report." Ephremael replied, his brother's glaring stare failing to fluster him. How much stronger having a purpose made him.

"I will hear your report…when I am ready, and not before." Olucard retorted, proceeding with his business as though Ephremael were not present.

"It is pertaining to an insignificant matter, a trifle really; surely not something to trouble the esteemed Olucard with." He said bitingly.

Olucard glanced up at the tone in his younger brother's voice and crossing his legs leaned forward on the throne, clearly displeased by the disturbance.

"Well?" he asked, his palms and fingers joined together as if in prayer as he rested his chin upon their steeple. "What is it that you are so very anxious to report?"

"It's about the Angel, Asielle." He said cautiously, wanting his tale to be as believable as possible.

"Who?" Olucard asked grumpily.

Ephremael wondered fleetingly if this report was even necessary, perhaps he could spare her from becoming part of his brother's knowledge entirely. But this faint hope was soon to be crushed.

"So, you discovered her name, perhaps you are not _completely_ useless after all." Olucard commented, not impressed in the least.

Ephremael questioned whether he should have revealed even that much. Somehow the thought of her holy name emanating from Olucard's vile lips filled him with a sense of perverse disgust. He shuddered with subconscious revulsion and Olucard quirked an eyebrow at him. Feeling his brother's watchful eyes dissecting him, Ephremael struggled to regain composure; his nonchalance was the only way to assure her safety.

"She is of no threat to us. We were mistaken in thinking so." He said calmly, hoping his brother did not know him well enough to discern the lies hidden in his words.

"You mean _you_ were mistaken. I believe it was you who first brought her unfortunate existence to my attention." Olucard said with his usual aloofness.

Ephremael tried not to let his relief at his brother's apparent disinterest show as he nodded in agreement as though shamed.

"Yes, I failed to see that it was just an illusion set up by the Bellavie, the girl herself holds little power." A blatant lie but he had failed to muster up a more subtle, less easily disproven one.

"The Bellavie? What have they to do with this?"

"Probably more than we realize…" Ephremael said under his breath.

"What was that?"

"I apologize brother, for I know as little about the Bellavie as do you. But the circumstances at Callion were surely their doing."

"That much I knew already. Are you suggesting that the Bellavie broke the Seal they were responsible for creating? And why would they do such a thing? And how, seeing as they are a race long since extinct?" his eyes were shrewd and calculating as he watched his brother's face alertly.

"Perhaps the magic of the Seal had weakened extensively over time and the combined power of three immortals in one place was simply too much strain for it to bear. Perhaps this is the same reason no words can be perceived on the Scroll?"

Olucard grunted, which Ephremael knew meant that he had no better explanation for events; he took this as a good sign.

"Did Anguilla find out anything more about the Scrolls?" he asked, eager to change the subject.

"It is not only the Scroll we obtained that is blank." Olucard stated bluntly. "There has been no progress in decoding them made by either side. I have assembled an elite team to…requisition the second Scroll. When both are in my possession, I expect results. But you needn't worry about that, your part in this grand endeavor has come to a less than climactic ending." He said scornfully, waving his hand in dismissal. "Be gone from my sight."

Ephremael bowed with as much courtesy as he could muster and glided from the room, letting the door slam indecorously behind him.

"How I despise that bastard," Ephremael muttered as soon as he gauged himself safely out of earshot. Sometimes he wondered why he had followed his brother's suit in descending from Heaven. What had led him to make that decision? Had he desired more freedom, less rules? Was it fear of an uncertain future? If he had not made that fateful choice, would he be with Asielle now? Or did her appeal lie solely in the fact that she was, as it were, forbidden fruit? Once tasted, would her allure vanish? These doubts plagued him, always before he had followed in his brother's footsteps without question, what would it be like to be pitted against him? And did he truly wish to find out?"

"It's not like you to be so pensive sweetling, what have you to think about?" Anguilla asked from the shadows of the corridor.

He feigned a smile as he turned to face her.

"I never worry."

Her teeth flashed white in the bleakness as she pushed herself indolently off the wall and emerged into the dim light.

"That's the Ephre I know." She said, smiling daggers.

"Has my brother commissioned you to keep an eye on me?"

"Now why would you think that?" she cooed, edging ever closer. She wore a low-cut sleeveless bodice and a long slit ran down the skirt, exposing her luscious legs. Golden armlets twisted like snakes around her bare arms and her dark hair glistened in the lamp light.

"What do you want, Anguilla?" he asked impatiently.

"My, my, what's with the temper? Can't an old friend stop by for a chat?" she widened her fierce crimson eyes in a perverse mockery of innocence.

"Nothing with you is ever that simple." He answered guardedly.

"Oh, I am just as without guile as that slow-witted Angel that you fancy, what was her name?" she threw one arm around a granite column and swung herself around it slowly, a vicious glint in her eyes. "Oh yes, Asielle, wasn't it? What a perfectly dreadful name."

Ephremael stiffened perceptively, instantly worried about how much she knew. Had she followed him to the island that night? Had she witnessed their embrace and the longing that had consumed him?

"You have a strange sense of humor, Anguilla." He said, his cool tone managing to not betray the anxiety gnawing away at him.

"You think so? No stranger than God's, I suppose." She took his arm and began to walk down the hall with him. "You needn't hide things from me, Ephre, I'm not one of your brother's stooges. You can trust me."

Ephremael stifled a harsh laugh, trust her? The very idea was ludicrous; did she think him so gullible?

"I trust no one, not even myself." He answered curtly.

Her laugh seemed less than genuine as it bounced off the walls of the corridor leaving a leering echo in its wake.

"Wise <u>and</u> devilishly handsome, just my type." Her lips were curled so far back that it almost looked like a skeletal grimace. "It's just such a shame that insipid little tart doesn't share my feelings."

I won't give her the satisfaction of a reaction, Ephremael thought, combating the anger that had flared to life in his heart.

"We both know you are not capable of feelings, Anguilla." He said sharply, wanting to be rid of her.

She looked at him balefully and in a shocked whisper said; "Why Ephre, that hurts, really it does."

"Stop calling me that!" he snapped.

"Heheh." She snickered, "Oh relax, you're so uptight." Her fingers snaked their way up to his taut shoulders. "Perhaps a massage is in order?"

He whirled around, violently twisting her wrists with the sudden movement.

"Do. Not. Touch me." He snarled, his patience worn thin.

"Rejection stings, doesn't it? Forget about her, I'll never reject you." She purred.

"Did you have something to say to me or not? I don't have the time for your mind games."

"My darling, we have nothing but time. But now that you mention it, I was so very eager to share the good news with you."

It was obvious she was baiting him but he asked anyways.

"What news is that?"

"Don't fret darling, that annoying little Angel is no longer an obstacle to our love."

"What ARE you babbling about? That Angel, whatever her name was, means less than nothing to me, as do you. I carried out my investigation as instructed and nothing more, my interest in her ended there." His irritation made his lies sound convincing and she hesitated, seemingly reevaluating the situation.

"Oh, is that so?" she inquired flippantly. "Then I suppose her incarceration won't bother you in the slightest." She pretended to examine her nails as she watched him stealthily.

"She's been captured?" his surprise was evident and he cursed himself for not keeping a cool-head. *That harlot has a way of getting under my skin.*

"Not by us." She said with a careless shrug.

"Out with it Anguilla." He commanded, now more concerned with the information than feigning disinterest.

"It's quite fascinating, really." She commented, "She incited Halliel to such an extent that he had her imprisoned. He's even more of a bastard than I realized."

He was stunned into momentary silence, which Anguilla undoubtedly noticed. Panic clutched at his heart, he had thought her safe. It had never occurred to him that she'd face danger from her own kind, had Lianzet betrayed her? And then an even more appalling possibility dawned upon him: was he to blame? Had Lianzet reported what had happened to Halliel, who in a rage had branded Asielle a traitor and had her locked away? The mere thought that he might be responsible for her suffering brought a rancid taste to his mouth.

"She's to be put to trial." Anguilla stated, clearly relishing his discomfort.

"For what crime?" he demanded.

"What does it matter?" she teased. "She's no concern of yours anymore."

He slammed her roughly up against the wall.

"I need to know." He said gruffly.

She appeared completely nonplussed, as if she'd been expecting this very reaction all along.

"Aren't you the curious one? Well, since you simply must know, I did hear a rumor or two." She paused, dangling the information just out of his reach, leaving him feeling frustrated and helpless. "They say that Halliel attempted to seduce her, and in apparent retaliation, she destroyed over half the gardens. Quite the feat considering she has no powers, wouldn't you say?" she glanced sideways at him with a knowing smile.

"Must be a testament to the power of a woman's fury." Ephremael suggested smoothly.

"Ooh, I like that answer. Lianzet was involved as well, you know. Ever the Champion of the Feeble, he couldn't help but to get in the midst of it. I wonder if that might interest Lord Olucard." She mused.

What did she want from him? Did she truly know anything or was she merely fishing, hoping he'd let down his guard and reveal the truth? He couldn't be sure, everything about her was artificial, each thought she uttered contrived, and her motives were an unanswered mystery.

"That is your risk to take." He said, deciding concise answers were the safest bet.

"Hmn…I suppose it would only upset him, and we wouldn't want that, now would we?" she winked at him and his hair stood on end as if trying to escape from his skin so as to be free of her sinister presence. He felt hunted by her every word and he didn't know how much more he could stand before his anger got the better of him and he snapped.

"Regardless, she is no longer a threat to us. In all likelihood, they plan to have her executed. The execution of an Angel…" she drew the words out, relishing the tension. "How I would love to see it."

Execution…the word pierced his heart like an arrow, turning his blood to ice. Such a loathsome act was surely not in God's wishes. How could they even contemplate putting an end to such a sacred life? How could Lianzet have failed so bitterly in his duty to protect her?

"You look pale, darling, let me help you to bed." Anguilla murmured, her eyes aglow as she reached for his arm.

Ephremael shook himself free of the spell his horror had cast upon him; for a moment there he'd forgotten the dangerous company he was keeping.

"Leave me. I think I shall retire for the evening."

"Fancy some company? We both know you won't sleep." Anguilla smiled sweetly. "You seem so very stressed, and I can be quite the comfort."

"I have need of nothing you might offer." He responded acerbically, "I simply have much on my mind." He turned to leave, more than ready for the conversation to reach its conclusion, but she was not yet finished.

"What's so special about her, huh? What does she have that I do not?" her voice was huffy, and he imagined a pouty expression upon her face.

Though the question took him by surprise his voice remained steady as he replied.

"I don't know what you mean." He kept his back turned to her, not willing to risk her glimpsing so much as a flicker of emotion crossing his face.

"You may fool your brother, Ephremael, but I am not so easily misled. You've much changed since your encounter with that fair-haired siren; don't think I haven't noticed it."

Was it that obvious? He had thought he'd hidden it well, his face an impenetrable mask against scrutiny. His mind raced to identify some word, some action that might have given him away but he came up blank. He had not been acting so out of the ordinary. Was it then merely some inventive jealousy that had led her to this belief?

"Just what are you accusing me of, Anguilla?" he asked flatly. "You do know how preposterous you sound? I have heard that jealousy drives a woman to madness but you have far surpassed madness and descended into severe delusions. Are you so unable to handle rejection that you must resort to such outlandish fabrications? I almost pity you."

He stalked off down the corridor towards his chambers, senses keen to any sign of her following, but there were none.

"Pity? I never thought I'd hear that word cross your lips, even in jest. I may have no proof yet, but I know that something is going on with you. I will keep it to myself, for now, your brother need not know. But do not underestimate me, Ephremael, if you make an enemy of me, you will not survive."

He listened to the fading of her footsteps before giving in to the thoughts crowding his mind. Was her information veritable? Or was it a trap to see whether or not he'd come to Asielle's defense? Was he being followed? A cursory glance assured him that he was alone but Anguilla's spies were insidious and easily overlooked. Amusingly enough, he might be safer within the walls of the Holy City than here amongst the comrades he had bled alongside for centuries. It was only a matter of time before Anguilla divulged her suspicions to Olucard, and while without proof Olucard would not act, Ephremael would certainly be put under watch, his movements restricted. And if what she'd said was in fact true, he couldn't allow himself to get trapped here, not when Asielle needed him.

However unwise it may be he realized that he really had no choice. If he assumed Anguilla was simply baiting him with false info and didn't act, only to find that he'd been mistaken…He couldn't bear to follow that thought through to its entirety. Asielle's life was at stake, there was no margin for error.

I'm coming, Asielle.

Interlude

Olucard watched as his brother's winged form vanished towards the horizon, as anger tightened his brow.

"I told you he'd go." Anguilla spoke at his side, all smug satisfaction.

"Follow him." Olucard replied tersely. "Bring your best men, if there is an opportunity to attack Itsukuenel, take it." He turned from the window and slumped into his throne, eyes narrowed in the darkness.

"You're taking his betrayal quite well. And here I thought you'd be angry."

He simply grunted in response.

"How quickly you utilize your own brother as a pawn; your

ruthlessness is a sign of a great leader." She twittered.

He lunged at her, possessed by sudden fury, his fingers wrapped tight about her neck.

"I believe I gave you an order." He snarled, teeth bared, "Now get out of my sight!"

He flung her from the room and slammed the door in her vexed face. Calmly, he returned to his seat, eyes forward into the future and mind calculating coming events.

"Little brother, you may have just given me the opening I need." He announced to the darkness, and throwing his head back he laughed, the smooth, rich tone camouflaging the wretchedness of his soul.

10 CHAPTER TEN

The walls were cold and damp, a dampness that clung to her soul like sap to a tree, a soddenness that she could not seem to shake. Hope shimmered in and out of existence, her mourn kindling for its extinguishment. Shoulders slumped and hair matted it seemed she'd been a prisoner for far longer than just three days, but then it felt like forever to her. How quickly she'd forgotten the tender warmth of the sun upon her alabaster cheeks, the crinkling of grass underfoot and the birdsong dancing through the breeze.

There'd been no outside communication, no solace from the all-encompassing loneliness, and she was beginning to feel forgotten. She passed the time restlessly dreaming, though her dreams were not much more welcoming than her waking reality. Always there was an unidentifiable voice calling to her, a corridor with no visible end through which she raced, searching for something that she could never find. The meaning of this dream eluded her, and she felt positive there was more to it than what she remembered.

She waited for her sentence to be passed, idly musing on what it might be. Halliel could not take back what he'd done, nor was he the type to admit to a mistake, so she already knew she would not be granted amnesty. Her suspicions were mounting more than ever before that she did not belong here, there was some other place she was meant to be; some other place that beckoned to her in her dreams and haunted her conscious thoughts by day. If she were to die here, then she'd never know this place, or the self that slept there. It was a morbid thought, she'd never really considered death before; she'd devoted countless thoughts to her beginning but never a one to her ending. Death was something mortals lived in fear of, it was not a fear for Angels. Nothing ever truly died, after all. Her consciousness might be lost to the wind and her form to scattered dust but her energy would remain, forever part of the Universe.

Still, to end her life in such a chaotic state would drench her soul in turmoil and angst and such intense emotions were what ghosts were born of. *Ghosts,* she paused on the word, the woman who'd appeared before her in what now seemed like another lifetime, what grief had trapped her here? What tragedy was she cursed to relive over and over again, and had Asielle been a part of it? Strange how the soul has no ending, while life is so very limited, one breath to begin, one breath to end. Would she ever see the truth as it was set before her? All these thoughts were pointless if she couldn't escape from here.

She paced the walls of the constrictive cell, palms fumbling along the moss-strewn walls eager to discover structural imperfections, breath bated whenever her fingers seemed to discover a crack. Her search was thorough and methodical but her findings disappointing, there was another layer of wall behind the first, getting out that way would require tremendous force and she still wasn't sure it was worth risking using magic. She turned her attention to the floors, which unfortunately were cobblestone as well, with packed dirt underneath, bolstering their strength. So then to the door she looked, and saw in it her only solace. But the door was as heavy as her heart and there was no budging it. With breath laden with despair, she leaned against its creaking resistance, the air escaping in strangled sobs. Her slender white hand slid through the bars, like a dove so strangely out of place, its grace dancing against the darkness. She wished her heart had wings so that she could send it far from this dismal place. There was no hope to be had here.

If I look, will I see you? She wondered, not even knowing who it was she wished to see. And the shadows reached for her and called her by name, and fear rose unbidden in her chest. For those seeking darkness, this was surely the place, but sanity once lost was hard to recover.

I cannot stay here.

"Let me go!" she shouted to the void, fully expecting no reply, her voice raspy from neglect.

The cell door creaked open and she stared with amazement unbecoming.

"Still, I find you here. Why, when you might've run? Are you so willing to throw your life away?" asked a voice from beyond the void.

"Who—" she knew not how to ask.

"Yes indeed, who. If you do not know, than I surely do not." Came the indistinct reply, neither clearly male nor female, it was without identity.

"An open door does no good unless one chooses to walk through it."

She stepped lightly to the cell door, peering beyond it into the darkness where a presence hid itself from view.

"Where are you?" she asked, one foot still lingering on the cell floor as if afraid to pursue the light it had so fervently longed for.

An arm gripped hers, nothing but a blur under the flickering lamplight.

"Come, this way." The voice commanded, tugging her forwards.

She balked. "Wait, who are you? Why do you help me?"

"Why does it matter?" it retorted.

She remained hesitant. "But, if I run--"

"Do not fool yourself into thinking you have a choice. Your imprisonment will only fuel the rebellion sparked in the hearts of the righteous, and bring about the battle for the control of Heaven long before its due."

"What do you mean? What has happened while I've been locked away?" she demanded, worry pinching at her voice.

"Your knight champions your cause, and he is quite convincing. Now, follow."

Dragged through the winding corridors, ever further from the stairs, she pondered the stranger's words. *My knight? I have no knight; a knight pledges loyalty to one and one alone…* Lianzet's ochre eyes flashed through her mind, what was it he had said? Not that it needed to be said, it was more than evident in his every action.

"I will protect you for as long as I am able, Asielle."

She couldn't recall when he'd said it, and she wasn't sure how it had been forgotten until this moment, but she remembered asking: "Why?" She hadn't expected a real answer, but he had given her one nonetheless.

"You are the only one worth protecting."

She hadn't known what he'd meant then and still didn't, but surely that constituted as a vow? So then, her worst fears had been realized, Lianzet had officially proclaimed war against Halliel, and he doubtless had company in doing so. The balance of power in Heaven had been shifted, and all for her sake? Oh this was terrible, she must hurry out of here, maybe once Lianzet knew she was safe, he'd call off this pointless battle.

"Please," she implored, "Take me far from here."

"It is as I intend." Came the reply, the grip on her arm unrelenting as the dim light.

The corridors became increasingly narrow as they forged through the darkness and Asielle wondered how such an extensive network of tunnels came to exist under the city. What were they for? Had God in his infinite wisdom created them knowing that this moment was coming? Had he foreseen her capture and even her escape? It was certainly not beyond his power, and Asielle preferred to think that everything had a purpose and that God was still watching over her, aiding her flight in his own unspoken way.

The ceiling dropped considerably in height and her undisguised wings scraped against the crudely cut stone causing her to wince. Up ahead came the faint whisper of rushing water, leading to even more speculation. The air was damp and cloying and dew clung to every hair on her body, causing her to glisten with reflected light. Her guide was steadily silent as they meandered through the dark into parts of the tunnel that retained their natural formation, crumbling rock walls and jutting shards of quartz haphazardly arranged. *The bowels of Heaven*, she mused. All this time she'd been unaware that a whole other world existed beneath her feet; she wondered if Lianzet knew. *Lianzet, please don't do anything foolish.*

"Your thoughts are so loud I can practically hear them," voiced her reclusive escort.

Startled, Asielle gaped at the shrouded figure.

"You needn't worry so."

"How do you know my thoughts?" she inquired, genuinely intrigued.

"It is not hard. You have not a deceptive bone in your body."

"Is keeping secrets not deception?" she asked, thinking of the Scroll which only she could seem to read, the forgotten voice of God that only she had heard, the apparition and her powers that she had kept hidden from her dearest friend.

"Nothing good would come of revealing those truths. You must know that." Her guide replied, as if it had indeed read her thoughts.

"Just who are you that you know of such things?" she was becoming increasingly frustrated by the lack of definite answers and beginning to question following this strange character any further.

"I am simply someone who does not like to see beautiful things caged."

"If I am a danger to those I care for do I not deserve to be caged?" she had been so long left to the cruelty of her own thoughts that to let them take physical form and emerge into the outside world was a relief she could not deny herself.

"Learn to love your powers and they will no longer be a threat. You think of them as a snake in the grass when in reality they are the wings to set you free. You are your only sanctuary." The hollow voice replied, as if its response made any logical sense.

Before another question could rise to the forefront of her mind, the expansive roar of rushing water overwhelmed her senses as the claustrophobic tunnels opened up into a spacious cavern. An arched opal bridge ran the length of the room with its towering ceiling glittering with precious gems. Phosphorescent moss provided the only illumination and yet the walls were aglow. Perilously close to the narrow bridge was the source of the cacophony, a majestic waterfall that shone lavender in the light. Its source was too high up for her to glimpse and it plummeted to an end far below where the tendrils of light reached. So struck was she by the inherent beauty that she felt a song of admiration welling up inside of her.

She knew that she should not give into it, but the urge was so very compelling. Just as her lips began to part with the promise of melody, her guide spoke.

"Ilcandasor, the Bridge of Holy Tears. Stifle the joy that burns in your heart, for this is a place of great tragedy. It was here that God lost his one true love as the price of power."

She was instantly alert, what nonsense! God was above loving only one soul, he loved all unconditionally, that was one of the things that made him more than Angel and man combined.

"She was much like you, Asielle."

"What absurdity is this??" she exclaimed, flustered, "and how came you to know my name? I certainly know that I did not offer it."

As if this 'thing' knowing my name is really the part I should be focusing on, she berated herself.

"How very ignorant you are of the origin of the one you worship; and yet even more ignorant of your own." It chided as it glided across the bridge as if weightless.

Asielle rushed to catch up to it and clung pleadingly to its concealed shoulder.

"No more riddles, I beg of you. Please tell me what it is you know about me."

"It is not something anyone can tell you; you must discover it for yourself."

"How?" her voice cracked with desperation, just one straight answer is all she needed, but the creature seemed incapable of giving one.

"There's nothing more I can tell you." It replied as it hastened across the last foot of bridge, where yet another nameless tunnel awaited them with gaping jaws.

"But you've told me nothing!" she protested as she followed.

"This is where I leave you, I can go no further." It paused, then added, "Wait here, someone will come for you."

What? Her mind couldn't process it quickly enough, but her guide was vanishing into

the darkness, it seemed unfair that no doubts plagued him, her, whoever.

"At least leave me with a name," she urged.

"Lysantha," replied the vanished form.

She tried it out on her tongue, "Lysantha? Is that your name?"

"I will take whatever name you choose to give me." The voice sounded close and she advanced tentatively back across the bridge, seeking its host in vain. There was no trace of the shadowy figure, not a footstep nor a shadow.

"That's not what I asked! Please, honor me with the name of my rescuer!" she begged of echoing darkness.

"I have given you all you ask for. It is only that you know not what to ask. Wait, and he will come. From this moment hence, he will always come for you."

"Who? No, please! Don't leave me here!" she implored, but it was pointless, whoever had led her to safety had vanished as mysteriously as they'd appeared, it was almost as though she'd imagined the whole thing; and now to wait in oppressive solitude for another anonymous stranger to arrive. She stole a glance down the foreboding tunnel ahead, where nary a speck of light could be perceived. She'd come this far, surely escape was well within her reach. How long was she expected to wait for somebody else to save her? Could she not hope to save herself? The shadows offered no answers and so she ventured forth, slowly and without expectation, casting a wistful backwards glance at the glorious waterfall, bereft of her gift of song.

Hands outspread on the uneven, craggy walls she stumbled down the tunnel with a grace undeserving of the word. Inaudible fears nibbled at the farthest corners of her mind as time slipped by, as time tends to do. Her progress was painstakingly sluggish and without means for measurement, and when she fell it was without warning. The sturdy ground abandoned her feet and she hadn't time to even utter a scream before she was deposited rudely on moss-covered floor several feet below. A faint light shown through the forest-green plants and she frantically brushed them out of the way, eager to shed light on her surroundings. The moss scattered easily beneath her fingers and soon the floor emerged. She felt her breath catch in her throat, the floor was transparent as a sheet of glass and below it floated endless spirals of pure orbs of lights in every imaginable color. They glowed and shimmered, casting iridescent light patterns, they burst into being like stars and shot through the darkness like comets. She reached out towards them longingly and they gathered under her palm, thumping against the glass in their eagerness to reach her.

"Magic…" she whispered, for this is certainly what it was, the only name that could possibly match this endlessly glorious creation. Perhaps it was this stream of magic that kept Itsikuenel afloat. So much concentrated power, and yet individually each orb seemed so very finite and fragile. This was not a place she was meant to see, the forbidden sanctum that lay at the heart of her world. She drew herself to her feet unsteadily and continued on, though her only wish was to enjoy the radiance beneath her.

She hadn't gone far before another obstacle presented itself, the tunnel forked up ahead, with three seemingly identical routes available. A small whimper escaped from betwixt her parted lips, it was starting to seem she would never make it out of this maze. Was someone even now waiting for her back at the waterfall to guide her to safety? She regretted disobeying instructions, how would anyone find her now? She whistled down each tunnel, listening intently to how far each echo travelled, but they were indistinguishable from one another.

"Which way?" she queried out loud, her desperation peaking.

"Which way?" echoed the tunnel on the left.

"Which way?" repeated the center tunnel.

"This way." replied the right tunnel.

She shook her head in disbelief.

"Is someone there?" she asked, but the echoes were merely echoes.

"I'm really losing it." She said as she stood at the entrance of the right tunnel, "Taking directions from an echo, but I have nothing else to go on."

It was as good a choice as any, she theorized as she took a deep breath and strode into the tunnel.

Ephremael

Dark shadows over clouds of pearl, moonlight reflecting crimson on luxurious wavy locks. The steady thump of wings colliding with the night air, the wispy clouds parted like curtains to allow him passage as if sensing the urgency in his flight. The fury that coursed through his veins was almost visible in its intensity and it lent him great speed. Rage was something he was made to feel and express, a sensation comforting in its familiarity, both explainable and tangible. The burn of hostility reminded him of who he was, an identity that had been thrown into chaos ever since his first encounter with Asielle, and which had remained mired in murky uncertainty ever since

I am Ephremael, Angel of Wrath, there are those who fear and loathe me, and those to whom I am their only strength. This is who I am and despite all the fluctuation in my life, it is who I will always remain. Though it was his gift to bestow wrath in the hearts of those who desired vengeance, he had never understood the emotion so well as he did now. He knew now what terrible wrath he was capable of, and if any harm had befallen Asielle, it would rise in him like an unquenchable thirst. They better hope she was without a single blemish, or he swore he'd rip off their wings one by one and stuff them down their gaping mouths.

The parapets of the city rose through the gloom to pierce the skies with their holy light. He glided between the clouds, using their haze as cover as he tried to form a plan. He had rushed here brashly with no consideration of what he would do once in enemy territory; he didn't even know where Asielle was being kept. He scanned for sentries and alarm bells rang through his mind as he noticed their suspicious absence. The Holy City was always well-protected, with pairs of sentries posted by each tower. Halliel, though arrogant, was always prepared against the threat of invasion.

So where then were the guards? Cautiously he circled each tower but there were no Angels to be found. Perplexed, he left his cloud cover and flew low into the city, stealthily landing in the shadows of the buildings. It seemed deserted, and apprehension clutched at his throat, squeezing it tight, if they'd moved Asielle somewhere he'd never find her; he knew not where else to look. As he stalked through the silent streets of his long-lost home, a remembered fondness rose in him. He had loved this place once, was it possible that he could again? And then he heard it: the unmistakable sound of battle.

A fight? His brother wasn't fool enough to attack the Angels at their stronghold, he'd tried it once before and it'd resulted in a horrific massacre that had greatly dwindled their numbers. After that rude awakening Olucard had changed tactics to favor stealth, in a contest of brute strength the I'rae would always have the losing hand.

Peering around a tower he surveyed the area, attempting to pinpoint the noise, and was drawn to the courtyard gardens.

Chaos had erupted in Heaven.

11 CHAPTER ELEVEN

Ephremael

The garden soil was inundated in blood, silver seeping into every crumb making the ground squelch with each footstep. The sharp clang of metal ripped through the cool night air, shredding the calm to pieces. Angels plummeted to the ground left and right, bodies streaked with blood, feathers raining down from the night sky like snow to a dreamer.

What was this that he had stumbled upon? He thought of the glee that Olucard would glean from this scene; without any influencing from him the Angels were destroying themselves. But why? His eyes lit upon Lianzet in the forefront of the fray, locked in bitter battle with Halliel and he began to make sense of it. Lianzet was unquestionably loyal to God and preferred order, there was only one thing worth more to him than law and that was honor. Halliel would've had to greatly breach the limits of his authority to provoke such an extreme response from the even-keeled Angel, and Ephremael recognized the brand of anger Lianzet wore like a badge on his face. It was the same animalistic rage that he had brought to bear upon him not a week hence, and he knew there could be but one cause. So, he was here for Asielle as well. *I won't let you be the one to save her,* Ephremael thought, *this time, I will be her hero.*

He slunk away, back into the cloak of darkness, not caring who emerged the victor of the squabble. If they killed each other it would mean an easy end to the war; without a clear leader to follow, the Angels would fall into disarray and Olucard would effortlessly achieve dominion over Heaven. What a horrible idea, what had ever made him support Olucard in his ambition to rule over all? When the I'rae had first been established it hadn't been about that, at least not openly, though he now suspected that had been his brother's agenda from the start. It had been more of an act of rebellion against Halliel, against laws that no longer needed to be followed without God to enforce them. It had been an expression of freedom and a declaration of doubt that Halliel was any more fit to interpret the words of God than anyone else.

As much as Ephremael loathed the idea of living in a Heaven ruled by Halliel, a Heaven ruled by Olucard was undeniably worse. What terrified him even more than this thought was the one that followed it: *Maybe I don't care, as long as I can be with her. I will accept whatever version of the world that allows me to keep her by my side.* He tried to shake himself loose of these thoughts, when had he morphed into this wussy adaptation of himself? Where was the icy-hearted man who cared for no one and nothing? Who had never felt the pulse of love through his veins? He was disgusted by himself, how could he have allowed that dulcet-toned beauty to change him so drastically? He tried to be angry with her, thinking: *This is all your fault, Asielle, you turned me into this pathetic wretch,* but the anger wouldn't stick. The conscience that had withered from neglect within him now sang stronger than it ever had before, its insistent hum invading his pangs of self-pity. Any thoughts he harbored about turning back now and leaving Asielle to her fate were quickly crushed and he begrudgingly accepted that resistance in this matter was futile.

He scoped the surrounding buildings for hints as to Asielle's whereabouts as his mind plagued him with another form of doubt. *I know that I want Asielle by my side. It's the only thing I've ever been sure of wanting, but what if what she wants is something very different? What DOES she want?* He realized rather sheepishly that he'd given very little thought to what she desired, only considering the fulfillment of his own longings. Could he assume that she wanted the same? They had said so very little to each other and yet he'd thought he'd understood her, identified in her eyes the same yearning for his lips pressed against hers that he had felt so strongly. Had it been simply his own pride, reflecting in her what he had wanted to see? He was no longer sure.

He shrugged it off; it wasn't like him to entertain such trepidation. Things weren't so convoluted, if she didn't echo his feelings now, then he'd just have to change her mind. *You hear that, Asielle? I don't care what you may think of me, I'll win you over, and I WILL make you mine, just you wait and see, I'll make you love me.*

A furtive movement in the gloom caught his attention and put him on guard. Someone lurked in the tall grasses just beyond the nearest tower, an unexplainably muddled form that could've easily been mistaken for a shadow by one with duller senses, wingless and foreign to the landscape. *Wingless*…this was indeed strange, for without the aid of flight the Holy City was completely unobtainable to those who dwelled on the earth below. It was not an Angel, nor could it be of mortal origin, so what then was this fellow intruder? He crept carefully closer, employing all the furtiveness he was capable of so that he became indistinguishable from the shadows through which he moved. The robed figure slumped down into the grass so that only its shoulders could be seen and Ephremael could hear a faint murmuring chant. Just who was this being, and what part did it play in the unraveling of Heaven?

As he drew nearer the mystery only deepened, the cloaked form was inconsistent, shifting forwards and backwards in time but never constant. It was seemingly solid, but the boundaries of its shape lacked definition, its edges blurred as if unsure where to begin and where to end. *What abomination is this?*

In a still stranger occurrence, the figure glanced up, and though no eyes could be seen, Ephremael could feel the full force of its gaze boring a hole right through to his core. He froze as a mouse in an owl's sights, unsure as to his next move. A spindly arm materialized from within the cloak's shadow and gestured towards the ground near where its feet would be, if it had any.

"She is waiting." Came a guttural voice, causing Ephremael to bolt upright with surprise. Not a foe, then. He advanced with every semblance of confidence till he stood not but a foot from the stranger.

"I've come for Asielle." He announced, jaw firm and voice unwavering. "Can you lead me to her?"

A nod like sludge being drawn to the surface through a sluice, a movement both painfully slow and murky.

"She is waiting," it repeated, arm outstretched towards the tall grass.

Ephremael looked carefully where it pointed, rustling the thick overgrowth out of the way with seeking hands he perceived a dip in the ground, and hacking the grasses with his blades an underground staircase was revealed. Musty air escaped from the open maw, treacherous cracks evidence of its abandoned state. He doubted even Lianzet in all his wisdom knew of this secret stair.

"Asielle…is down there?" he turned towards his mysterious accomplice for further guidance only to find that he was very much alone. Not a trace of a second presence could be discerned, not a blade of grass disturbed, not an imprint in the air.

An illusion? He mused. Illusion or not, a path now lay before him and the choice was upon him whether or not to take it. Was this meant to lead him astray, or was there some other force at work that sought to preserve Asielle's precious life? Could it be a messenger of God? He laughed in spite of himself. God, indeed, what did God care what became of his Angels? He was an absent parent and only slightly more so now than when his words had ruled the Heavens. *We have no need of God,* he thought bitterly as he stared into the unrelenting darkness below. He had no other ideas where to look for her, and he adamantly refused to turn back now.

Hold on Asielle, I'll be with you soon. With a final glance at the glorious moon, he descended into the perilous glom with blades held at the ready.

12 CHAPTER TWELVE

Ephremael

It was dark, far darker than even the farthest corners of his mind. He did not fear darkness, and why should he when it constituted the core of his very being? Usually the cloak of night brought him comfort, the black blanket of sky conspiring to hide his sins while the sun's bright rays brought them back to stark realization. However, this was not THAT darkness, this crepuscule offered nothing, it was cold and cloying and clung to his skin as if it were a physical presence and not merely the absence of light. It fostered unease in his already wary senses. He could not be further from Heaven were he in Hell itself.

He felt along the icy stone walls for a torch or wall sconce but his searching fingers found nothing. He struggled to recall the incantation to summon light; though his magic was powerful it was as dangerously unsteady as his temper. The spell fizzled in his palm leaving a scorch mark on the delicate skin. *Of course,* he thought, *even Heaven's shadow rejects me.* He stared resolutely into the tunnel ahead with his piercing turquoise eyes alight with inner fire. *Reject me all you want, but I'll keep on coming.*

It seemed to him that the adumbrations were mocking him as he advanced through the gloom, one careful step after another. The tenebrosity never abated, even for a mere morsel of a second and yet his eyes failed to adjust to the bleakness. If there were booby-traps he stood no chance of evading them. He felt like he'd somehow slipped through the cracks in feasible reality into some netherworld that slumbered just below it. It certainly wasn't natural, but it would require some strange sort of magic to create this maddening atmosphere.

He drudged dutifully along, never feeling any closer to his goal. For all he knew he hadn't moved an inch and was still stuck right where he'd started. How would he ever find his way back? The stairway had closed up behind him, if it had ever really been there to begin with. The whole thing was exceeding strange, that there should be such an obvious invasion route leading to the very heart of Heaven that neither Olucard nor the Angels knew about seemed way too far-fetched. Halliel never left weak spots exposed, the only reason Ephremael could think of for not defending this place was that it defended itself; which was not a thought Ephremael particularly liked to entertain. What lurked down here in the recesses of Heaven with him? Had God placed a celestial watchdog here long ago that even Halliel feared? Why include this tunnel at all? He hadn't an inkling of what it could possibly mean, all he knew for sure was that this absolute darkness irked him greatly and he wanted to be gone from here as hurriedly as possible.

He tested his wings but the domed ceiling ambushed him, rubbing the top of his wings raw. He winced and ducked down, he hadn't noticed the proximity of the ceiling to his head and for the first time in his existence he found himself wishing that he wasn't so tall. Somewhere up ahead he heard a strange crying most definitely not Angel in origin that made his bones cave in as if weakened. *That seems about right,* he acknowledged, every instinct informing him of an encroaching battle.

"Couldn't make it easy for me, could you God?" he asked the oblivion, "Not even to rescue one of your own beloved children?"

At the outermost edge of his senses he almost heard a chortled: 'no.'

"Well then, give me all you got. Don't hold back because it'll take all you have to keep me from her." he asserted as he closed in on the source of the eerie wailing.

Asielle

There must be an end to this darkness; every shadow has its counterpoint in light, so too there must be an answering brilliance to this gloom. She wondered what the black hid from invasive sight, knowing that secrets are best kept in darkness. Just as the dungeon hid evidence of best forgotten memories and kept them from ever coming to light, here also was a place the light deemed unworthy of its grace. Did she belong here with the other deviations forsaken by illuminated truths? Maybe she wasn't meant to leave this place after all, but even shadows crave light. To walk once more in the glowing embrace of the Sun she would gladly give up her wings.

Walk with me, I will be what you cannot see, sighed a soft wind against rough-hewn walls. Her inner dialogues were becoming indiscernible from outer surroundings. There were words not heard but felt, strangely without origin but they fit undeniably, like seams to the shadows. The dark moaned within her blood turning her breath faint as whispers. Tendrils of sense were fading with every step and she got the distinct feeling that time for her was running out, running away from her. *Stay,* said the shadows, *Stay and forget the difference between light and dark.* To forget wouldn't be so bad, she thought, but forgetting erased nothing from existence. Even if she were to forget who she was, the rest of the world would still remember. It wouldn't affect reality at all; forgetting wasn't a real solution to anything.

Up ahead, anguish waited, she could hear its mournful cry, another creature misplaced by light. Instead of fear she felt unquestioning pity, and the wish to restore light to this soul kissed by darkness. To ease suffering, was that not the true call of an Angel? It was so close she could feel the pain radiating off of it like heat, pungent and unforgiving. Like salve to a wound was kindness to a stranger and she had much to give.

She had almost forgotten her ability to see, so accustomed was she to the darkness, and she felt sure that time down here was as lacking as was light. It did not matter now if she'd chosen the correct path, the very act of choosing made it the right one. Her steps light as falling snow she glided forward on feet that had no fear of ground. The cry hungered for respite just where silence meshed with shadow and became one. She did not sense evil, only frailty. Palms outstretched as though embracing the void that exists both within and outside of us, she sailed ever further into the darkness which was growing steadily inside of her.

Her fingers touched upon what her senses deemed to be splintered bone, rough-shod and crumbling as if under the strain of a great wind.

"The song…can you not hear it? Maddening in its persistence, threatening to devour all sanity."

She pressed her palms against her ears in sudden pain, the voice was grating, churning her every pulse, a frenzy of chopped motion. Was this a creature driven to lunacy by the relentless darkness?

"I hear no song." She admitted, "I can hear nothing but your voice. Do tell me who you are?"

"Who is anybody but a definition placed upon the indefinable? Once was I shunned, two times forgotten, but sacred was I in the star-fueled fire. I am nothing more than the failure of what I attempted to be."

A soft rustle in the darkness as ice brushed against her skin like the touch of lost life. Fingers stabbed at her, scratching her skin with their ragged edges, more like pointy twigs than fingers, yet even more devoid of life.

"I am a shadow cast into shadows. I am but one of many discarded fragments."
"Discarded? By whom?"

Hands raked across her wings, trembling with fury eager for an outlet.

"Wings…Wings!" it cried melancholily, an unearthly howl tearing from its throat as she was shoved roughly backwards.

The creature's skin crackled with its every movement as it slammed her back against rock. For the first time she noticed a fetid smell about it, the undeniable scent of decay.

"Here have I been longer than there are days. You are still pure, still pure; there is no place for purity here. No place."

Dead flesh slapped against her face, moist and scabby, a tongue spreading foulness behind it like a snail. She quivered at the malevolence unmasked and pushed back against this driving force. It was then that she heard it, faint as regret at first and just as sour; quickly building into a shriek so plaintive that her ears began to bleed with pity. It was a song for the lost, and a song that became lost the more it was heard. Full of strangling grief powerful enough to split the Heavens in twain, perhaps it was this song that was the true prisoner. It wreaked havoc with her mind, she could see everything and yet nothing, she had never known that a song could be anything but beautiful.

Crows with eyes like prismed beetles swam through an endless fog where light became sound and sound became fire and all that was and ever would be burned and perished in unrelenting fire. The bitter notes of the song fanned the flames. With eyes that reflected a past not yet seen, she looked past the sea of longing to a star dead in its birth where a forlorn wind whistled riddles unanswered. She felt her consciousness sliding away sluggishly as sand in a jammed hourglass as the song rose in timbre and the creature began to glow in eerie light.

It was skeletal and terribly twisted, a mess of mismatched gangly limbs amassed in clumps of overgrowth. Its spindly legs were not structurally sound enough to support and yet it moved with fluidity unrivaled. Veins protruded from parchment-like skin, a roadmap of its pain and suffering, knobby and crusted as scabs. It had no eyes to speak of, nor a recognizable face, only a hollow where a face may once have rested; with gaseous orbs of green fire floating about in a disorganized fashion. Without a mouth she could not understand how it spoke, or where it might conceal a tongue, which only made it worse. There were growths on its impossibly wide shoulders that dropped sadly behind its back in a pathetic mimic of wings. It was unimaginably grotesque and waves of revulsion struck her as her eyes took it in. Whatever this creature had once been, there were no clues to its former self left behind now. She was desperate to understand the hatred that had so corrupted it.

"Do you have a name?"

"*I am nobody's shadow. Not anymore. Unclaimed, I am unclaimed! Neither light nor dark will take me.*"

"You poor thing…not even a name to call your own." She was inexplicably sympathetic to this ghoulish fiend that clearly intended her harm. There was just something strangely familiar about it.

"I'm looking for the way out; wouldn't you like to leave this place behind? Come with me, let's go together." She hadn't intended to make that offer, yet it had sprung from her lips as surely as though she had, and there was no taking back words once said.

It laughed, a painful sound rattling against the cage of its battered chest.

"*The only way out is in. The outside world does not exist for me, far too much light. Your wings, once broken, will forget of flight. It's only painful if you remember. And so…I will help you to forget.*"

It advanced with claw-like hands extended and Asielle fumbled in the near-dark for her blades.

"I am not yet ready to forget," she exclaimed, brandishing her blades in front of her face protectively. "But nor do I wish to fight you."

The creature hissed violently, jaw unhinging in a horrendous grimace. It curled its decaying fingers around one blade and shrieked with a fury that shook the cave walls and caused Asielle to teeter off-balance. A momentary rush of burning air coupled with a rancid smell forced her eyes shut and when next she glimpsed her swords it was with no small measure of horror.

They had wilted, or maybe melted was closer to it, they were as twisted and tangled as the creature's decrepit spine and even more useless. Her blades, forged in the fires of Heaven to withstand all but an Angel's fury, now reduced to nothing more than shrapnel to fuel the war. The creature continued to advance. It had no need of a face to convey its leering countenance; it was evident in her mind's eye.

She tried to back away but there was no room left to run. Magic, then, was her only recourse. With a gentle hum held low in her throat she flared her palm outwards and let a fireball loose at the gangly fiend. It passed right through the creature, solid though it was, and continued off into the tunnels, leaving behind it a trail of smoldering air. Again the creature laughed.

"*No power backed by God can cause me harm. You are without hope, little Angel, just like me.*" The sinister chuckle made her spine collapse in on itself and she buckled to the ground, paralyzed by preternatural fear. What more could she do?

"Please," she tried. "Please, I must stop this war."

"War? There is no stopping war, there is only interrupting it with peace. Cease your struggles; leave your soul to the keeping of shadows."

Its hand drew nearer and nearer to her face and spread darkness across her mind.

"No…" she protested weakly. "No…"

The dark was so very strong, and she so very weary. Her only remaining weapon her will and it was fading from her rapidly. She could not resist much longer.

Ephremael

Even before the fireball came whooshing around the corner he knew that he was no longer alone. Someone else had engaged the eerie wailer in combat and he felt slightly gypped. Whoever it was better not be aspiring to become Asielle's savior. He cared little if they shared the same goal, he would not stand for competition in this matter.

He whispered low onto his blades and they hummed to life in response, fiery runes appearing on the flawless metal. That spell, at least, worked. He had never been more ready for a fight, the oblivion of these mind-warping tunnels made him eager for the errant song of violence. He sprinted into action, body slung near to the ground and muscles taut with apprehension. The lingering trail of celestial fire provided some guidance through the darkness and it was through their favor that he glimpsed the beast. His stomach recoiled in disgust at the deformity that confronted him; never had God's grace been so absent from a creature.

"Wretched soul, I'll deliver you the freedom you long for!"

He faintly registered the body slumped against the walls but his concentration rested solely upon the nightmarish abomination. Such grotesqueness simply begged to be destroyed, and he was more than willing to oblige. His body was in action long before his thoughts registered it, lithe and sinewy as the shadows from whence he came. He leapt upon the gnarled shoulders and crouching down he stabbed at the gaseous orbs, hoping to disable the monstrosity. The blades met with no resistance, scattering the green vapors for less than a minute before they reassembled themselves. With an infuriated howl it whirled around, claw-like fingers stabbing at the air as it reached for him.

He leapt nimbly out of harm's way and regarded his foe warily, searching for a weak point. He couldn't imagine a heart residing in its hollowed out ribcage, indeed it seemed to have no organs at all powering its movement. He'd simply have to annihilate it, one limb at a time. He darted towards its floating left arm, the creature was insanely fast, but Ephremael was faster still and his blades connected with a resounding clang as if against metal. He felt the jarring reverberation in his bones as his arms shook with the force of the impact.

His effort was rewarded by little more than dents in the skeletal frame, small scratches that oozed Shadowlight. Though perhaps he should have been discouraged by this, Ephremael was not the type to give up easily on anything.

It swung at him angrily and Ephremael ducked with ease. The poorly aimed fist hit the jagged wall and the creature yelped in pain. Before he could react, it had sunk its fang-like teeth into his arm, causing blood to gush forth. Ephremael hadn't even realized that it possessed a mouth. It gnawed its way through to the bone, teeth gnashing with vicious intent as its tongue lapped up the fallen blood greedily. He tried to force it off, prying at the clenched teeth with bare hands but it only dug in all the deeper. Ephremael plunged his blades into its scrawny excuse for a neck, wedged the tips in its pointed shoulder blades, and brutally slashed at every inch of exposed flesh to seemingly no avail.

Then suddenly the creature let out a scream of indisputable anguish and released him. Ephremael stumbled back, his upper arm a mangled mess. Even having no notion of pain he knew the wound could well be lethal. His howling foe clutched at its gaseous head with both hands as though trying to contain an explosion, as it spat blood frantically from somewhere deep within the haze.

"Dark one! Dark one! It screamed incessantly. *You, who abandoned God! I taste your sin!"*

My sin? Ephremael wondered, uncomprehending. He remembered the foul thing's teeth as they gleamed with his blood that it had seemed so very hungry for and which now lay in discarded pools on the cave floor. *The sins are in the blood?* Inspired, he coated his blades in the blood that still steadily seeped from his wounded arm. The blades shone with the mixture of the silver blood and the Shadowlight with which they were imbued.

Shadowlight was the highest power of the I'rae. Invoking it awoke dormant powers while greatly enhancing existing ones. It made its caster far more powerful than any had right to be, transforming them in unimaginable ways. Its power was unpredictable and dangerous and came with great cost, draining the life-force of the caster in exchange for temporary power. When not invoked it was almost benign in nature, adding magical protection to weapons and armor and emitting a strange light that somehow burned black as shadow, thus its name.

The metal sung in his hands as he hurtled towards the shrieking menace and drove the tainted blades into its concave chest with a hiss. The scream that spewed forth was so piercing the walls trembled and chunks of stone rained down upon them. Its loose-hanging skin reacted to the blood as if it were acid, sizzling and smoking as it ate away at the bones underneath.

Ephremael was taken aback, he hadn't expected such a severe reaction, never before had he seen his blood cause more harm than his blades. Unholy creatures were said to have adverse reactions when in contact with beings of holy origin, such as Angels, but he wasn't really Angel anymore. Still, not understanding it made it no less effective, and Ephremael resumed the battle with the renewed vigor that comes of tasting success.

His strikes were swifter and stronger than lightening and his accuracy unerring. Within moments the creature was incapacitated beyond reasonable movement. Trails of flame spontaneously erupted, following the lines of blood as they zig-zagged across its hideous form. One by one its arms clattered to ground as the blood ate clear through to the other side and it fell to spindly knees. Its utterances of agony were too much for Ephremael to bear. He stood over it with blades raised overhead, preparing for the killing blow when he felt a slight tug on his ankle and someone whispered:

"Don't…please, Ephremael, don't."

Startled, he glanced down to see Asielle clinging wearily to his leg, her body splayed out on the hard ground as though there was no more strength left in it. Her garments were tattered and torn, her face streaked with dirt and her luxuriant locks matted, but still her beauty was a radiant light in this darkness. *Is there nothing that can extinguish her beauty?* He wondered, awestruck. Then a sense of joy such as he had never felt before overcame him, she was here! He'd found her, and she still lived! Without thinking he scooped her up in his arms and held her close, burying his face in her tangled hair and dreading the moment when he'd have to release her. His foe was momentarily forgotten, all he wanted in this vast universe was this woman and here she was. What need had he of anything else?

She was too weak to protest, hanging limply in his arms like a child's discarded doll, her feet dragging behind her, but Ephremael barely noticed, so overwhelmed was he by euphoria.

"What-what are you DOING?!" she exclaimed, furious. "Put me down at once you brute!"

"Hm?" he glanced down at her face and saw that she was livid with anger. Apparently, he had overstepped his bounds yet again.

"Fine." He sighed, reluctantly relinquishing her.

To his horror she crumpled to the ground and he knelt worriedly by her side.

"My sweet Asielle, what have they done to you??" he demanded, incensed beyond the point of rational thought. "I'll kill them! I swear I'll kill them!"

"Calm down," she said, propping herself up unsteadily on one arm. "It will pass; just let me rest a moment." Her earlier anger was gone, replaced by sudden relief at no longer facing this darkness alone, and a curiosity that demanded to be sated.

"What are you doing here? How did you get here?" she inquired.

He stared at her blankly, it seemed quite obvious. "Why, I came for you, of course; to rescue you. Is there any other reason to trespass upon this dreadful place?"

She shook her head in dismissal.

"I just don't understand you at all. You knowingly entered into enemy territory to rescue one of your foes?"

"No." he replied patiently, "To rescue the maiden that I l—"

THWUMP!

His forgotten nemesis head-butted him from behind and he felt a rush of coldness creep into his bones with its contact. Almost as though he was possessing the creature's own scrambled memories he was plagued by a host of negative emotions in quick succession: forlornness, betrayal, defeat, rage and desperation all flooded through him, accompanied by a twinge of pity at all this faceless ghoul had endured. He felt a strange kinship to it; it too felt betrayed by God.

"It must be put out of its misery, Asielle. You can't possibly think that it wishes to continue like this." He said as gently as possible.

"I know." She responded to his great surprise. "But, please, let me do it. It has experienced enough violence."

He nodded in agreement, though he was unsure how she could accomplish anything in her current condition. She struggled to an upright position and with feeble hands clasped she began to sing a song far different than what he'd heard before. This song was beyond mournful in tone and her words flowed through him like tears. As she sang her wings floated out from behind her, glowing with holy white light of such blinding brilliance that a mortal's eyes would have burst.

The creature wailed along with the song as if it had once known the lyrics though they were garbled on its invisible tongue. It was a truly haunting melody, soulful and wistful; speaking of things that once lost can never again be recovered. As Asielle's melodious voice rose to a tender high note that Ephremael doubted any human might hope to reach; he began to perceive a change in the creature. It began to glow softly, its twisted spine slowly realigning, the dead remnants of skin rejuvenating at remarkable speed. Lost limbs regenerated and scars miraculously disappeared. Its long-lost face began to emerge as the green orbs dissipated and Ephremael discovered with shock that this creature had once been beautiful.

Forgotten wings unfurled from newly supple shoulders like golden sails in their majesty. By song's end, the creature's true identity lay revealed before them: an Angel. He was horrified, is this what became of those who foreswore God? Was this the fate that awaited him?

Though clearly a Seraph, the nameless entity was unlike any Ephremael had ever seen. His regal wings, for it was clearly a male, spread far wider than Ephremael's own and shone with golden light like the sun. He was straight and tall, with glowing sun-kissed skin and flowing ivory curls that slept in an invisible breeze around his crown, mimicking a halo. There were strange runic symbols seemingly carved into his flesh that pulsed with blue light. His face was possessed of such unearthly beauty that neither Angel could bear to look right at it. The song drew to a climactic close, to her credit Asielle did not falter once despite the astounding transformation occurring in front of her.

It knelt down before her, giant stature bowed in gratitude.

"It has been countless ages since anyone saw me as I truly was. I am but a shadow of my former glory, yet in your mercy you have redeemed me. There are others like me, scattered to the four winds. I pray that you show them the same kindness that you have shown me."

The Seraph stood with great dignity as light began to flow from inside it. The light wrapped itself around his unprotesting form like a climbing vine, all the while growing brighter. Soon no features of the newly unmasked Seraph remained exposed save his beautiful opalescent eyes. Asielle choked back a sob and reached for the fading creature.

"Do not mourn me, my child. Too long have I remained chained to darkness. It is time for me to return to the light." Its voice echoed in their heads. The light-cloaked body exploded into thousands of orbs of sapphire light, scattering like fireflies to far reaches of the tunnels where they gracefully departed existence.

Tears rolled down Asielle's face and Ephremael felt ill at the sight. He gathered her into his arms, wanting only to comfort her, though he knew not why she cried.

"You released him from his suffering, why do you cry?" he asked, soothing her furrowed brow with his thumb without forethought.

Her reply was muffled by tears.

"You would cry too, if you had a heart to break."

He recoiled, stung by the harshness of her words.

"I tried to save him, only to destroy him instead." She continued, looking up at him with luminous violet spheres.

"Is that really what you think of me? If I am heartless, then my heart surely does not know it."

Heartless, he'd been called many things in his eons of existence, but never before had words had the power to feel like grievous wounds. Barbs buried in his heart, tightening around it and puncturing the only softness in him that still remained.

"Why are you here, Ephremael? Haven't you caused me enough trouble?

I don't need you."

He knew her anger wasn't really directed at him, but still it pained him. He couldn't help but think that she hated him.

"I don't doubt that's true." He answered with as much composure as he could muster. "However, I very much need you, and that is why I am here, Asielle."

She looked at him as though he was crazy and he realized how insane this all must seem.

"You need me…" she repeated. Had anyone ever said that to her before? What did that even mean?

Mistaking her silence for rejection, Ephremael elaborated. "Asielle, I came all this way for you, I know that I am the last person you hoped to see in these tunnels. I wish that I was Lianzet right now almost as much as you must wish it."

Her head snapped up at the name and she tried to get to her feet only to have her knees give way beneath her and send her crashing back to ground. Ephremael was at her side in a flash, eyes rife with evident concern and she felt a bit guilty for her callousness towards him.

"Lianzet, did you see him? Is he all right?" she inquired, frantic.

"He fights Halliel for your freedom." Ephremael responded, jealous at the loving tone with which she said Lianzet's name. Would that she would say his name with such tender care.

She looked as though she might cry again as she desperately tried to get her legs to cooperate.

"No! I must stop them! If they fight, they will destroy Heaven!" she stubbornly rose to her feet again and again only to collapse back to the floor. He couldn't help but to admire her dogged persistence.

"Here, let me help you." He offered, reaching his hand out to her.

She eyed it suspiciously; clearly she did not yet trust him. He had never worked so hard for a mere smile in all his many days.

"How many times must you fall before you accept that you need my help?" he asked, frustrated.

She glanced upwards at him and he nodded, assuring her that it was alright. *You can trust me,* he beseeched with his eyes, afraid to utter the words out loud lest they backfire upon him like every other attempt at communication seemed to be doing. She grudgingly took his hand and he hoisted her to her feet. Her balance was still shaky and as she started to teeter he positioned himself so that she fell against his shoulder. Her body stiffened upon contact with his and he savored the brush of her soft skin against his arm. He smiled at her encouragingly and she relaxed ever so slightly. Then she noticed his right arm, seemingly for the first time, and a look of alarm spread across her face. He'd completely forgotten about the wound.

"Your arm!" she exclaimed.

He shrugged nonchalantly. "It's just a scratch, it will heal."

"We're not going anywhere until we treat that." She said adamantly, trying to disguise the disappointment she felt at the postponement.

"You barely have the strength to stand," he pointed out. "You're of no help to anyone if you cannot even walk."

"Sit down, I'm treating it." She said insistently.

"If you use any more magic, I'll have to carry you out of here." He chided, and then grinned at her candidly. "Actually, that doesn't sound half bad, go ahead and treat it then."

She glared at him. "Don't you dare take pleasure in all this."

He held his hands up in mock surrender. "Oh no, I wouldn't dare, milady."

A deep sigh escaped from her as she closed her eyes tight in concentration, holding both hands out towards the shredded arm though she threatened to topple over with each passing second. He placed his left hand upon the small of her back to steady her, delighting in the warmth of her. She didn't seem to notice so focused was she upon her spell.

As magic began to flow from her hands to envelop the wound in comforting light he marveled at the incredible amount of magic that she harbored in her petite frame. His arm began to recover a recognizable shape as an addicting heat spread through his veins like the rays of the sun upon one once frozen. As the muscles remapped themselves he felt an increased strength in them, as though she had not only healed his arm, but improved upon it too. Was such magic possible? But then again, everything about this girl seemed an impossibility; perhaps by now he should not doubt that she was capable of miracles.

Her magic spent she fell into him and he instinctually caught her. Her eyelids fluttered trying to stay open, apparently the spell had taken more from her than he was expecting. He cursed himself for getting injured; his own carelessness had caused this. He wrapped his arms under her knees and cradled her against his strong chest; at least one positive came of all this negativity.

"Your arm…" she murmured drowsily, "I must…finish healing it."

He shook his head. "You've done more than enough, you sleep now. Leave the rest to me."

She peered at him through lashes so lowered she could barely see.

"Lianzet…he needs me. Please, Ephremael, take me to him."

"I would do anything just to hear my name upon your lips." He whispered, but she was already out, her gentle breaths like fairy kisses against his heart.

He watched her as she slept in impossible perfection, his eyes greedily devouring every detail of her face to be used as fodder for his waking dreams. He didn't want to share her with Lianzet, nor with any other. To have her to himself for all eternity he could not think of a thing he would not do. Maybe he could just stay here for a while, cherishing the moment, after all he may never again get this chance to hold her so close.

She would never forgive me, and that I could not bear. Resignedly he headed back the way he had come, ever mindful of the fragile treasure that he carried. His footsteps more sure than his heartbeat as he carried her from the darkness which threatened to consume them both.

13 CHAPTER THIRTEEN

Asielle

Someone was carrying her, holding her tightly and securely against their beating heart in a way that would have made her feel safe under even the most dangerous of circumstances. *Lianzet,* she smiled sleepily, but it was not Lianzet's golden eyes that stared down into hers with such smoldering affection. Instead she gazed up into tumultuous tropical seas, their peaceful color hiding a craving to devour her whole. She shuddered involuntarily and the eyes crinkled into a smile of relief.

"You're awake," said a decadently rich voice, "How are you feeling?"

"How…should I be feeling?" she muttered, closing her eyes again. The world was spinning in front of her, what little of it she could see, anyways.

"Well it has been quite a harrowing day. I really wish you hadn't expended so much of your power on me, you had me quite worried you know."

She fought her way back to consciousness and focused again on the face floating above her: crimson hair that shown with inextinguishable fire, chiseled jaw and handsome features. His wings flared out behind him both glorious and fearsome to behold. She knew this face; she'd just misplaced the name.

"You're not…Lianzet." She managed, defying the weariness that lingered on the edge of her senses, threatening to shut her brain back down.

He raised his eyebrows, clearly unsure as to whether or not she was kidding.

"No…" he drawled smoothly. "Come now, you know my name."

"Yes, but…it is lost to me. At the moment, I cannot recall it…forgive me?"

"You're serious?" His face was a frenzied mix of conflicting emotions, concern and relief and just a hint of calculated cunning.

"I do know you." She said reassuringly. "It is all just a haze in my mind." She rubbed at her temples as though that miniscule movement might cause everything to somehow fall back into place. She looked down at her feet dangling in the air. "Do you think perhaps you might put me down now?"

"I don't want to." He replied flatly.

This was not the answer she was expecting.

"You're afraid I'm too weak to stand?" she hazarded a guess.

"Something like that." There was not a trace of emotion in his response.

"I assure you, I am feeling quite alright now."

Unable to think of a legitimate reason to maintain his hold on her, the handsome Angel rather reluctantly set her down. She faltered a little and he was quick to stabilize her.

"Thank you." She smiled, and watching his face she thought she spied a glow spread across his features as though she had never before smiled upon him.

"What happened to me that I am so very weary?" she asked.

"Well," he said slowly, "as much as I'd love to refresh your memory, now might not be the time. If we remain here any longer we're tempting fate."

"What has fate to do with any of this?" she inquired, befuddled.

He smiled roguishly. "I should think fate has quite a lot to do with it. Believe it or not, you're an outlaw of Heaven."

"An…outlaw? Me?? It's not possible…I disobeyed God's holy order?" she was in shock, how could she forget something of that magnitude?

"Yes well, Halliel didn't quite approve of our union." He remarked casually.

"Excuse me?" she shook her head vehemently. "I may be a bit muddled, but I certainly would remember something like that."

He gave her a lopsided grin that she found rather pleasing. "It was worth a try."

"My being an outlaw, is that also untrue?" she asked hopefully.

"Somewhat. Halliel did have you thrown into prison and slated for execution." He held out his hand to her. "Come."

She took it cautiously and he pulled her forwards through the darkness.

"I can't believe Halliel would go so far. You were the one who released me? It must have been quite dangerous."

"Yes, quite." He flashed her a smile so brilliant she could espy it even through the gloom.

"Um…so might you tell me your name?" she asked.

"You'll remember." He said confidently.

"Are you always so cocky?"

He paused as if considering it. "Hmm…yes, pretty much."

How obnoxious, she thought, *still he did risk much to come rescue me.*

"And what of Lianzet, why did he not come with you?"

Her rescuer's broad shoulders seemed to tense at mention of Lianzet's name.

"He employed a less…stealthy approach." He said cryptically.

There came a soft rustling in the tunnels up ahead which she knew to be wind but her less astute companion clutched at blades hidden within his sleeves warily. A faint and unmistakable glow came from them: Shadowlight. This man was I'rae.

Panic gripped her as she fumbled for her own blades, only to find nothing but the shattered remnants; she had no weapon. She knew instinctually that she hadn't the strength to employ her magic, and she very much doubted her ability to outrun him in her current beleaguered state. But surely it would be easier to lose him in this twisted maze of tunnels than above ground where the moon would betray her position. She could see the tendrils of light fast approaching in the distance; it would have to be now.

"What do the I'rae want of me?" she asked simply, keeping her tone even.

He stopped walking.

"I don't know what you mean." He answered so coolly that for a second she thought perhaps she was mistaken.

"You are I'rae." She stated.

He turned to face her, seemingly unperturbed. "And what makes you think that?"

"None but I'rae use weapons of Shadowlight."

He glanced down at his sleeve and carefully tucked the blades back in. "Maybe I confiscated them." He suggested smugly.

"No." She was assured of her suspicions now; he wore darkness about him like a cloak. How could she not have noticed it before? "Tell me why."

She wrenched her hand free from his and took a step backwards into the black night of the tunnels, and he in turn took a step towards her.

"Asielle…" he reached for her, "Don't do this, please."

"Why would a lone I'rae trouble himself with the rescue of an Angel, his mortal enemy? If you had simply let Halliel kill me you'd have one less Angel to fight."

He seemed upset by this. "I would never allow that to happen. Now, come here. Let us leave this foul place."

She took another step back.

"Why?" she repeated.

"Come here, and I'll show you why." He purred invitingly. The downy hair on the nape of her neck stood up.

She paused long enough to make him think that she was debating the idea, and just when he seemed sure her intention was to oblige him, she turned and fled into the tunnels. His footsteps thundered behind her as he angrily called out her name. She ran as fast as her numb legs could carry her, blindly dashing through the void, blind terror nipping at her neck with the prospect of what he might do to her once caught. This fear fueled her frantic flight and soon she could hear his footsteps no longer. She crouched down in the darkness to catch her breath, listening intently for any signs of her pursuer, but all was quiet.

She was at a loss as to what to do next, her captor might wait by the exit for her return, and yet if what he'd said were true, Halliel and his loyal posse awaited at the other end of these tunnels. She had no real reason to believe his words, but on this matter she did without question. Danger lurked down whichever path she chose to take, and it was so very easy to become disoriented in this bleakness. She stood, and closing her eyes tried to sense the correct route to take. Though the I'rae was alone, in a way she felt far more threatened by him than by whatever army Halliel could muster. There, then was the answer.

She turned in the direction she judged the prison to be and started jogging towards it, not fully convinced that the I'rae had given up his pursuit. He didn't seem the type to bow graciously down to defeat. Though she heard nothing to indicate his presence, she felt him close by and began to run again, her tired limbs protesting bitterly.

"Stop!" a firm grip was upon her wrist and she was forcefully twisted around to face him.

His turquoise eyes were raging fury and she flinched as though he might strike her.

"Don't ever run from me." He snarled. She beat upon his chest with her free hand.

"Let me go!"

"Never." He said shortly, grabbing her flailing hand and pinning it against his chest.

She was utterly terrified of this man, though she could not pinpoint just why.

"Please…can't you let me go?" she pleaded, changing tactics. "I am of no use to the I'rae."

He exhaled sharply, clearly frustrated. "Silly girl, you still don't get it. I did not come for the I'rae, I came for you. I will always come for you."

She looked up at him, and somehow his sincerity frightened her far more than a blatant lie would have. She had to try just one more thing.

The fire was in her heart and mind long before it reached her hands, burning in her palm like a molten brand. She held the spell for as long as she was able, till her throat was rubbed ragged and her eyes began to water with the strain. The flames laced out from between her fingers, snapping out at him, slithering up his arm like a snake. He released her out of surprise and she was running again, though she knew not how she had the strength. Everything she had was put into that last surge of resistance, and though in truth she only made it a few steps, it felt to be forever.

He grabbed her and she twisted and fell, landing roughly on her back with wings outstretched beneath her. He fell with her, catching himself on his elbows and propping himself up as he loomed over her, their chests nearly beating as one, with his wings coating them in shadow. Every line on his face bespoke of anger and she began to tremble. *It is only because I am so weary,* she told herself, even knowing it was falsehood.

"I thought I told you…never to run from me." He hissed through clenched teeth, and she turned her face from the rage in his eyes.

With a touch more gentle than she had imagined he was capable of, he turned her chin back towards him, holding it steady so she was forced to gaze into his captivating eyes. She was unclear of his intentions; this man was like a puzzle that she had no hope of solving. His purpose was unfathomable as the sea. He was enigmatic and daring and the less she understood him the more mesmerizing he became. He was fixated upon her face in a way that made her want to squirm like a trapped bird, but she could not find it in herself to move.

Slowly his free arm found its way down to her waist and wrapped itself around her tightly. He pulled her up into him and their bodies collided, the warmth of him dangerously intoxicating. Her heart began thudding in her chest and she could feel the heat rising in her face. He dipped his head down towards hers and their noses brushed. Voltage surged through her in a painful shock as though she'd been struck by lightning.

"L-let me go." She stammered feebly, panic seizing at her throat.

Without a word he gently set her back on the ground and removed his arm from her waist. He stood and offered her a hand up, which she courteously accepted, being too weak to refuse, and they stood facing each other in the dark.

"Thank you." She said, her voice quivering with bit-back apprehension.

His face was inscrutable and for one moment of rushed relief she thought he was going to let her go. She took a hesitating step back and with the fierce speed of a bracing wind he slammed her against the nearest wall, knocking the breath right out of her. Before she even had the presence of mind to summon anxiety his hard mouth was pressed against hers with a passion that defied every thought that she had ever had about love. His lips were surprisingly warm and inviting, and even though there was such vigorous fervor in the way he sought to meld her lips with his, she could still tell that he was holding back.

She didn't want to enjoy it, but her emotions held the reins. After all, she had never really been kissed before. She melted into him like warm honey, his mouth claiming her as his own as surely as though she'd been branded. It was a scorching, dizzying rush, leaving her every nerve frazzled and frayed. Her blood sang with the pulse of electricity and for a moment, one blissful moment, she felt invincible.

The moment soon ended, he pulled away from her and she felt a grudging sense of loss. Without a trace of a smirk he spoke.

"I will never let you go. Not ever."

Ephremael.

It all came flooding back to her then, and fury overtook her. Her hand flayed his cheek like a whip, leaving red splotches in its wake. The spell of that moment was broken and discarded as all unwanted moments are, aborted before they've even the chance to become memory.

"Ephremael!" she shouted, teeth grinding with inward-bound frustration. "You have NO right! No right!"

She had meant to sound angry, but instead she sounded just like what she was: lost and confused. Her anger towards him was tempered by her inability to recognize her own feelings. She was of two minds about it, at once both furious and another contradictory feeling that she could not name. Contentment? Relief? She didn't need to look at him to know that the inconsistency was evident on her face.

"You remember. Ah well," he said with a careless shrug, "I suppose permanent memory loss was too much to hope for."

She scowled at him. "I may have forgotten who you are, but I could never forget what you are."

"Harsh." He said snidely. "I am just as you are; it is only my choices that make me I'rae."

"Our choices are all that matter, Ephremael. What other means do we have to define who we are?"

"Hm." He mused. "Then…what does my choice to be here say about me?"

She was still, her existence diminished like a doused flame.

"I wonder the same thing." She whispered as soothingly as susurrus.

She realized that she was afraid. As much as she longed to leave this place behind, the chaos that awaited her on the outside was just as daunting. What kind of state would she find Lianzet in? Was she prepared for the sight of maimed Angels? Prepared to see the gardens of Heaven soaked wet with blood? What if she could do nothing to stop it? The fire in her heart was all but spent and the war only just begun. She knew war, knew it intimately, and yet never had it tasted so sour on her tongue. It had never been so unclear who her enemies were, she was accustomed to sides clearly defined, but here the lines were blurred. Friends became foes and foes became friends, it was a very backwards experience.

"Why do you hesitate?" he asked, bringing her back to herself.

"What can I do…to stop this?"

He shrugged. "Maybe it shouldn't be stopped."

"How can you say that?" she asked, aghast.

"Do not be angered. I simply meant that sometimes the only way to end a war is to fight it out. It's well past the point where it could have been avoided."

"I must stop it. It's because of me that they fight…every death that occurs is upon my head."

"No, Asielle." His voice was stern and his gaze steady. "This battle would have come to pass with or without your influence. Halliel's corruption needs addressing, and the Angels cannot hope to win against the I'rae as long as they stand divided. Heaven is long due for a change of leadership."

"And what of the I'rae? What of their involvement?"

"I came alone." He said simply. "The I'rae will do what they must to survive."

"So I see. You are a traitor born. First you betrayed God and your own people and now you turn on the I'rae as well. Is there none to whom your loyalty is unyielding?"

He didn't seem offended; doubtless his restless spirit was something well-known to him. Perhaps he wasn't fit to be a follower, or else he had yet to find a cause he believed in enough to remain faithful to.

"I pledge my allegiance to none, and my loyalty only to you."

The blush was on her neck before she could think to stop it and she hastily covered it with her silken tresses. They shimmered like lost moonlight in the gray.

"You say the strangest things."

He smiled intriguingly, "Is that a bad thing?" His tone was teasing and his eyes playful.

"I have yet to decide." She took a measured step back towards whence they came only to be stopped by a hand on her arm.

"I hope you're prepared for what you will see up there. It is not the Heaven you remember."

"I am not ready, but still I must go." Her face was misleadingly serene.

"Then, let us go together." He said, his tall, lithe frame towering over her.

"I suppose even your company is preferable to facing this alone." She said sardonically.

He grinned back at her, clearly not daunted. "I suppose that's good enough, for now."

Her thoughts moved along with them as they walked back through the tunnels, now side by side in polar opposite of their first traversal. *Together, an I'rae and an Angel. What will Lianzet think?*

Ephremael reached for her hand in the darkness and she let him, needing someone to stop her from slipping back into everlasting night. Down here, maybe sides didn't matter, everyone was cast in the same shadow. *Down here, we are all lost,* she thought. *He lost himself purposefully just to find me.* She regarded him studiously; hoping if she peered hard enough the mask might crack and allow the truth to shine through. *But why? Why? What could you possibly hope to gain from this?*

A daunting thought reared its menacing head as they came around the final corner and the exit stood revealed, framed in pale moonlight. *He couldn't know about the Scrolls, could he? How could he?*

"Well, here we are." Ephremael said, stopping just short of the door, bathed in the silvery light. Every fiber of hair was aglow, floating gently about his face as pools of moonlight gathered in his crystalline eyes. Her gaze lingered a little too long on the magnificence of his form and he grinned at her haughtily. In this light it was easy to forget he was no longer sacred.

"Having second thoughts?" he asked.

"About what?"

His voice was sultry as he replied, his throat coated in velvet.

"Why don't we forget about Lianzet and the others? Let them fight their war, I could use some more time alone with you."

The mixture of horror and disgust on her face made him chuckle wryly and she wondered if he said such things only to get a rise out of her.

"You're despicable." She grumbled as she pushed her way past him and up the stairs to the world she'd left behind.

She paused on the final step, the moon full on her face and the clattering of swords in the distance in harsh discordance with the peace of the evening.

He couldn't know…could he?

14 CHAPTER FOURTEEN

It was a strong longing. The longing to make things right and he found it irritating. He was not looking forward to Lianzet seeing him and Asielle together. The pain of their last encounter still lingered in his bones; and he was quite sure Lianzet would rather kill him than Halliel. He thought about snatching up the pretty little Angel next to him and absconding into the night with her. There was bound to be somewhere in this vast world a place unpatrolled by Angels and beyond the scope of the I'rae's spies. A place where they could be together, hidden from the judging eyes of the world. If there was such a place he would rest his wandering spirit and bask there eternally in her presence, just to take her away from all this strife. To shield her from the ugliness of war, he told himself, though he knew that wasn't the real reason. Lianzet would only interfere; Ephremael knew that he would not be allowed to remain at Asielle's side once Lianzet was involved. *If we were alone, truly alone, I could make her love me.* He slyly peeked over at Asielle and she narrowed her eyes at him with suspicion as if she could sense the impurity of his thoughts. Shamed, he looked away, that fantasy would have to wait.

Wings unfurled like glorious sails in the wind he stood before her, majestic and proud. *Let her see in me that which I hide from all else. That which is uniquely me and therefore easily wounded. May her light define her and cast me not into shadow. May I find her ever seeking my embrace. Like a psalm to my lips her sacred name be, never felled by false intent. I will hold holy all that brings her joy and bequeaths unto me a smile. For in her my star is matched and where her bones are laid to rest you will find me weeping still. Take not her from me, dark swan of sorrow, for my heart would not rise again. For it is in her absence that I am extinguished.*

The echoes of long-forgotten vows came reverberating to the surface of his clouded mind. Once he had scoffed such prose and its tribute to a feeling that could not exist for him. How he longed to be able to scoff it once more. There was a thunder in his ears and heart that could not be ignored for something so simple as fear.

"Asielle…" he started, but she was already miles from him though she right before him stood, and he lapsed into pained silence once more.

"We will find him." He offered reassuringly, and she replied without turning.

"I'm not so sure that I want to."

"Huh?" Faint hope sprang to life deep inside his chest.

"Do not misunderstand; it's only that…I'm so very frightened of what I might see. Lianzet…is really all that I have."

Ephremael's face contorted with the sting of that remark.

"Well, whatever we might find, I will be here besides you."

"Mm." Was all she said.

It's a losing battle, he thought glumly as he took her by the hand and dragged her towards the site of the earlier conflict.

There was nothing there, though the indisputable remnants still remained, great pools of shimmering silver blood and plucked feathers floating serenely in their tides. Broken fragments of sword tips lay scattered freely about and Ephremael stooped to examine them as Asielle stood frozen in awestruck horror. The abandoned head of a spear glimmered at the bottom of a generous blood splatter, its shine eerily familiar to him. He picked it up, carefully turning it over in his palm and holding it to the moonlight to see past its silver camouflage to the secret buried beneath.

His blades gave an answering call as they recognized their counterparts before Ephremael himself did. The dark glow was unmistakable. Shadowlight. Then…the I'rae had finally made their move. Had Olucard had him followed? He stood hastily, shoving the shard into his pockets where it lay hidden, humming faintly with ominous power.

"Ephremael…what happened here?"

Her face was blanched as snow and her eyes teary, though she offered him a sad little half-smile as if sensing his inherent concern.

He was slightly surprised by her response, after all, all Angels were warriors born.

"You have seen battle before, have you not?" he asked.

"Many times." She brushed the tears away with feigned indifference. "But somehow, I never quite get used to it."

"You are really not like the other Angels, are you?" he said without forethought. *Such a gentle, incorruptible soul, how has she survived this long war unscathed?* His desire to protect her purity grew ever more pronounced; somehow he must find a way to shield her from the ugliness that most surely lay just ahead.

"Why do you say that?" she queried softly, "You think I'm weak, don't you? I know…that's what they all think of me, and perhaps I am, in some ways." Her gaze held him captivated, her huge eyes aglow with trembling light. "But, my tears don't make me weak. You'll see, I am…I am more than just my sadness."

As he looked at her for the first time he noticed a strange sort of hollowness that wavered just below the surface, and he realized in that moment that she was just as alone in her way as he was in his. His reaction and impulse were one and the same; in one defiantly quick movement he cradled her head with the back of his palm and drew her against his chest, wrapping his other arm around her back to keep her close.

"Yes," he murmured soothingly, "Yes, I know dearheart." He breathed deeply of her scent as he absent-mindedly stroked her fine satin locks.

She allowed herself to be held, perhaps needing the comfort just as much as he himself did.

"I'm beginning to think…that you are all I've ever wanted, Asielle. And I never even realized that I was wanting for something."

She pushed away from him abruptly, shattering the moment as it fled to the dimly-lit recesses of memory. His straying hands had mussed up her glimmering locks and she hastily rearranged them.

"Why do you insist upon saying such very strange things? I can't quite seem to grasp you."

His smile was reminiscent of a sharks, all teeth and menace. "I am a poor editor of my thoughts. I can't seem to help but say what I mean. I do believe myself quite easily understood, but…you have to want to understand me."

Her eyes turned distant and cold as she shrugged off his words like a cloak grown too warm.

"Why would I ever wish to understand the disturbed mind of an I'rae?"

His smile was tender still, as if oblivious to the hatred thinly disguised by her words.

"Well, whether or not you care to understand me, I very much want to understand you."

"I am not for you to understand." She said, as her eyes wandered across the empty space, seemingly devoid of all life, a ghostscape.

"Where is everyone?" she murmured under her breath.

"I was wondering the very same. Where would they have taken the wounded?"

"Baukutet…" She was in flight before the name finished falling from her perfectly parted lips and he followed without a thought; knowing that for the rest of his life he'd always follow where she led.

Halfway across the gardens it happened, like a sheet of cold wind through his mind a chill came across him with the sudden unquestioning comprehension that they were being watched. A dark silhouette flitted across the moon, hurtling towards Asielle with a speed meant to kill.

He didn't warn her, zooming to her side and scooping her into his strong arms and out of harm's way with an agility that he had never before been so grateful for. He felt the impact behind them and shuddered at envisioning the pain it would have caused Asielle. Turning to face their attacker he found himself face to face with an I'rae, for the first time an enemy instead of a comrade. It was just yet another reminder of how rapidly everything was changing. He knew this I'rae, of course he did, they'd fought side by side in many a battle, though they'd never really been friends. Ephremael had never been the type to have friends. He supposed that it ran in the family, Olucard didn't have any friends either, only pawns.

"Ephremael, so it is true, you really are a traitor."

Ephremael said nothing, simply placing himself protectively in front of Asielle, who looked extremely perplexed by the whole exchange.

The I'rae peered past Ephremael, examining the Angel in a way that made her fidget uncomfortably. He turned a calculating eye to Ephreamel.

"You betrayed your family…for this?" He gestured dismissively at Asielle as though she was merely an occupied space not worth acknowledging; just another obstacle in the way of achieving his dreams. It was not so long ago that Ephremael had looked at her with much the same view.

"Soratis, what are the I'rae doing here?"

"That's really none of your concern anymore, is it, Ephremael?" He wrenched his spear from where it had burrowed into the ground and whirled it expertly. "I never liked you, Ephremael. You've always thought you were better than the rest of us. But I never figured you for a traitor; you've never been more than your brother's mindless puppet." He sneered at him. "If not for Olucard, I would've slain you long ago."

"I am better than you, and I'll prove it." He drew his short blades, gleaming with Shadowlight that opposed the moon. Asielle grabbed his arm.

"Don't. We have no time for this, we must find Lianzet."

He disliked the notion of saying no to her, but he knew that in this case he had no choice but to refuse. He could read the bloodlust fuming in Soratis's eyes; he would not back down from this fight till it was sated.

His opponent laughed, a sound as harsh as the cawing of a crow as it muddied up the silent air.

"She's even got you taking orders, eh? How far the mighty have fallen." The self-indulgent smirk on his face marred his otherwise seamless beauty.

"This cannot be avoided. I'm sorry, Asielle," he said apologetically, although his heartbeat trembled and quaked with the thrill of the fight.

She took a step back as though accepting of the inevitable truth, and Ephremael advanced towards his adversary, making sure to stay between him and the vulnerable Angel.

"You'd better hope that you kill me, Ephremael, because if you don't, I'm going after your little…pet."

Ephremael was in his face before he'd finished speaking, a fearsome rage festering in his clear, vibrant eyes.

"You shouldn't have said that," he hissed as Soratis staggered backwards, a blade protruding from his shoulder.

He stared at it incredulously. "When did you--?"

His question was cut off by the metallic whisper of Ephremael's second blade tearing towards him. There was a resounding clang as he blocked it with his spear.

"You won't catch me off-guard a second time, Ephremael. All I need do is land one hit; your speed won't protect you forever."

He pushed Ephremael back, and Ephremael used the resistance to wrench his blade free, his heels grinding into the fertile ground as he skidded to a stop three feet away. Soratis launched himself at him, hoping to catch him off-balance. Using his entrenched back heel for leverage, Ephremael sling-shotted towards his oncoming opponent, the impact of their collision causing the nearby buildings to quake. The blades shrieked with terrible fury, the cry of harpies on the battleground, as every feather quivered to life. Radiant they were, with splendor undescribed as they prowled side by side with stealth, with the spillage of blood forever on their minds. Their thoughts, however impure, did naught to tarnish their glory, though their thoughts were besmirched. Pride burned on their faces like a brand in the night, coloring their every movement. All this waiting was more agonizing than waiting for sand to sift through an hourglass to Asielle, whose eyes darted back and forth like mad in a fruitless effort at prediction.

Ephremael, in his turn, was relishing every moment with keen fervor and his opponent seemed similarly inclined.

"After craving this moment for so long, it is such a shame to have to end it so soon, but unfortunately, I have other engagements to attend to."

It was with a smirk that Ephremael met this challenge, every conflict in his life he had met head-on, this had always been his way, and it would continue to be so.

"Brave words uttered with such cowardice have no bravery to them."

"Laugh while you can. I will have your head, Ephremael, and what a fine trophy it shall make."

"I rather like it where it is."

Soratis's hand was glowing, an eerie shadowy flame that was far from natural, sucking the energy from the air until it became still and lifeless. Like prodding a dead thing Soratis continued to draw upon energy that wasn't there for the taking until his eyes turned bloody with the effort. Ephremael was not daunted, preparing a hastily constructed barrier spell though knowing it was his speed that he must rely upon. Daggers of pure Shadowlight descended upon him in a flurry of menacing shrieks as if the Heavens themselves were pouring down a rain of wrathful destruction. It seemed so blasphemous to corrupt a force made to feed creation and fuel new life into a source of redoubtable death.

The barrier spell held as well as could be expected, though in several places the dagger points protruded into the shield, stuck halfway through their flight. The second flurry would be stronger, he knew, and his counterspells were too weak to do much good. As long as he remained trapped in one place Soratis maintained the upper hand. *Let him believe that he has won,* Ephremael thought, even as the second volley commenced and he could feel the barrier weakening. Soratis was looking very pleased with himself as the first of the Shadowlight daggers penetrated the protective shield to pierce through Ephremael's foot, as solid as a dagger of Uthicon and still more painful. Ephremael took the hit with grace, his expression barely registering it. *If it all were to end here, there'd be barely a ripple against time. But I'd rather be the ripple who affects change slowly than the wave who forces change through its might.*

Sensing an opening, Soratis moved in for the kill, leaving Ephremael with just the opportunity he'd been waiting for. Like a gust of wind against a slamming door he was upon his prey in an instant. Lethal and quiet as flame his interlocked blades cut a bloody swathe through his opponent's armor, mutilating the exposed flesh underneath. Soratis fumbled for a counter, not realizing that the battle had been already won. With a quick twist of his wrists, the blades were freed of their fleshy prison, humming with Shadowlight as though sensing how near was a bloody ending rife with the finality of death. Soratis never saw him move, never felt the pain until it was long past fatal. His head rolled from his elegantly tapered neck and hit the ground in a slow-motion silvery splash. Ephremael's blades were sheathed before it finished rolling. He wasn't too proud to admit he was proud. Vanity was costly, but denial far more so.

Feeling suddenly abashed, he turned to face Asielle, expecting to see a sort of reprimanding dismay and judgment undisguised. His heart registered her absence long before his sight did and he experienced a gripping sort of panic hitherto unknown to him.

"Asielle?" Her name caught in his throat, lacking its normal sweet fluidity.

How long ago had she gone? He had been so focused on the fight that he'd almost forgotten that she was there, though it had all been for her sake. She was out there somewhere, alone in the midst of this mayhem, and he condemned himself for his negligence. He knew that she had gone after Lianzet, which perhaps made the separation that much worse. There was no telling what dangers she may encounter, he was more aware than most that the I'rae employed vile trickery in their tactics, as far as they were concerned there were no rules to warfare, and they played dirty if at all. His sense of accomplishment over his victory evaporated like the morning dew when faced by the overwhelming might of the sun. He had sworn to protect her, to make her safety his priority, and already he had fallen short of his promise.

He felt the shame creeping upon his face and the urgency to remedy the error he'd made prompted his feet to action. He had been bereft of Heaven for half a millennium now but the memories were still there, the layout of the Holy Kingdom as intact as the day he had left. He knew every inch of that cobbled walk, every flower with petals spread invitingly. No matter how far he'd strayed, his birthplace was an imprint upon his very soul and he wondered now how he could have ever beared to leave it. His feet flew with a speed that his dormant wings envied and he spied apocryphal glimpses of her around every corner, seeming portents of some disastrous end. With every step his fear increased till it boiled at the surface like lava.

When he found her there was an instant washing over of relief twinged with the bitter twang of remorse. Her wings were curved downwards with grief, their lustrous shine dampened by the shedding of tears. Back bowed over the fallen Angel she wept, her hair glistening with beaded light. He had found himself running to her side, fueled by an overpowering and subconscious need to be with her. But he stalled his exuberant approach as her sadness blew through him, shaking him to his core as a strong wind through a slender sapling not yet firmly rooted. She didn't react to his presence, seemingly numb to the world still going on around her, it was as if all life had stopped, and with it all awareness. There was a wrenching of the self palpable in his chest, as though all color had suddenly drained from his world. There was a fear too, of breaking the reverent silence, the nagging sense that maybe it was not meant to be broken. His whisper was all trepidation, her name breathing slow life back into starved lungs.

There was no response, no acknowledgment, and he almost questioned whether or not he'd actually spoken. He tried again, more assured now of his own voice. A plaintive wail, tenuously stretched upon the chill breeze was his only response. He reached out to touch her, half expecting her to shimmer away like an approached mirage but she was solid and warm with substance. The frailty of her garb did little to disguise the tremors that wracked her willowy frame.

She spoke with the mournful uncertainty of a child who has just witnessed first death.

"No matter how much I may sing, I can never bring her back."

He peered over her shoulder at the face she so lovingly nestled. Disappointment and relief created a bitter bile cocktail at the back of his throat as recognition hit him hard. It was not Lianzet, as he had hoped, yet also feared.

Baukutet's golden locks waved gently around her face, giving her the semblance of life with their lent vibrancy. Her beauty was so intact that Ephremael expected her eyelids to flutter open. This illusion was torn asunder when his gaze flitted downwards to a body wracked with bloody gashes and stained by memories of loss. She had fought bravely; the proof was in her many defensive wounds, her robe weighed down by blood. Her left wing was crushed beneath her, ragged and awkwardly splintered, the frayed feathers giving the pretense of age. Still, her face was serene, an offset to the violence that had spawned it. Shimmering opals blanketed her skin, sparkling with purity and the concentrated misery of their innocent host.

Trouble seems to follow you, doesn't it? Asielle regarded him through tear-blurred sight as if his thoughts were audible. He shrank back, not liking to feel so revealed. His vulnerability around her was something he both loathed and feared. He longed to escape from these feelings that tied him down, tied him to her, but returning to his old self scared him more. That husk of a man missing any shadow of desires, the very thing that makes man a man. But then, he wasn't man, he was Angel, supposedly above all such desires, all desires but love apparently. Love…what did he know about love? He who had been created to only love God, and then turned against that love. Would he turn too against these immured feelings that threatened to bloom in his chest with fierce fiery light? Looking at her delicate, upturned face he found it hard to believe or even imagine, but at one time he would have responded with equal incredulity at the thought of ever being separate from God. Did he simply lack faith? The faith to believe in anything outside of himself? If he could not remain faithful to his very maker, could he ever hope to remain faithful to her who carried a world in her eyes, a world he wanted nothing more than to save and treasure? And did it really matter what would happen, could happen in the future? The future wasn't now; she was breaking in front of him _now_, needing his comfort, _now_. NOW was all-important. The future, whatever it may be, would have to wait.

"Asielle…" He knelt down beside her and allowed her to weep as he kept a watchful eye on the skies above. He slipped her ivory-smooth hand into the encompassing warmth of his own and squeezed gently, giving comfort through constant presence. Mourning was a luxury of time, and he was well-aware how very little there was to spare, but every superfluous second there was he donated to her indulgence.

The rain was coming down. There was nothing in existence where the presence of God could be felt so clearly as in rain. He felt the guilt of God's disapproval like a weighted shroud of shame. Even in his absence God was judging. That's where the hatred had begun, in the constantly perceived judgment, when God was meant to be acceptance and loving approval. He had never felt that from God, perhaps because he simply couldn't believe in the concept of a truly unconditional love. Unconditional love was love devoid of all judgment, and what was God but the High Judge of the world that he'd created? If he was to be loved, he wanted there to be a reason behind it, for it to be based on some merit of his. If God truly could love with equanimity, then he was no different than any other of God's children, he could never gain more love for himself, nor lose any, so there was left nothing to strive for. If Asielle was to love him, as he hoped with all his soul she might, it would be due to his earning that right, that privilege. To his mind, what good was a privilege innate instead of earned?

But the whirring of wings was like locusts in the sky and the folds of his robe dripped with silver blood. Any semblance of safety evaporated like the misty shroud of dawn when confronted with the rising might of the sun. He reached for her and tugged her to attention. Retreat was a word he did not care to associate with, but in this moment it was what was needed. Silence the only worthwhile reason. It was a call to the fading of the light. Solace for the keeping. It was a strain to find the words to goad the action but find them he did. Burdensome on the tongue though they were he squeezed out their utterance like clay through a sieve. Her voiceless acceptance was a mercy, perhaps the only one afforded of the evening. The shimmering of fallen tears gave way to the shimmering of wings as they ghostly crept towards the dawn. Each moment more tedious than the next as time hung taut between opposing forces who were not yet aware that they opposed. Somewhere in the alleviated darkness lay the waking world that dreamt of the slumber of Angels. The grasping fingers of mist clenched down upon reality and all sound was muffled in its wake. What song could reach them now, and would it have words?

He knew not where he led her, only that he must get her away, borne away with the nightscape that receded from the golden hues of a blood-soaked morn. How could anything be the same again, now that irrevocable steps had been trepidatiously taken? The world would reflect upon this day, he grew quite certain of it. For once he was glad that God was not present to witness the murder of his once-beloved children. Stone-cold silence, without the whisper of a word. No guidance from above and little from within the caged heart. Solemn thoughts took hold in that murky stillness between the here and the now. Even silence was forgetting there was a name it bore.

"If you shed but a tear over me, I would return to life just to spare you from more."

She was watching him quietly, but he was unreflected in her eyes. *Could I be the one to reach her now?*

"Asielle, where have you gone to? Come back to me…"

15 CHAPTER FIFTEEN

Asielle

That voice…who's calling to me? Please…I do not understand, what is it that you want from me? The Scroll…? Here? But I…how am I even moving?

Her surroundings came into focus slowly, as though she'd just arisen from a long sleep. Someone was holding her hand, firmly guiding her…but where? There was an unpleasant stickiness caked to her palm and she stared, dumbfounded. *It's…silver…*Recognition was a sickly pleasure. *Oh…Baukutet.*

She unconsciously grasped the pendant around her neck, wondering guiltily if her possession of it had somehow sealed her fate. She had most likely perished in an attempt to attend to the wounded. She was…She had been, the most pacifistic of Angels, wishing harm unto no one, but war was never so discerning, it took life even from those who sought to save life. A sudden surge of rage coursed through her blood, the I'rae had struck down an unarmed healer. It was unthinkably barbaric to her mind that any Angel of God should have strayed so far. The I'rae were truly cut from a different cloth. Even, Halliel, tainted as he was by his many sins, would never treat a foe so ignobly. They truly are just as demons, and demons could not be left to rule the world. Yet what could she, a mere feather in God's wings, do to stop them?

Then it came again, an incessant cacophony challenging the boundaries of her mind. She knew that it was only to her that it called. There was an urgent need for her to validate its existence. She moved towards the sound, or rather, the sound moved her, seeming to emanate from within and without simultaneously. It was a voice she had never before heard and yet recognized. She knew without a doubt that it beckoned her to a grand and undiscovered destiny, which she already doubted her ability to fulfill. The call filled her world, she could hear nothing, experience nothing else. It was all-consuming, there was no other way for it to be.

Heavy wading, a blank canvas upon which the world was scrawled, she was everywhere and nowhere at once. Ceasing for no one, and yielding to nothing. She was a nothing in answering to something. Something beyond being, beyond conflicting wavelengths and existential incongruities. It was the space between, which could not be named, <u>should</u> not be named. It was not for her to name, it surpassed labels. The sound grew louder, plaintively pleading in tone, filling all the cracks in her reality until it was seamless. The din had her heart racing and her pulse fevered, light spread bony fingers before her eyes and all her senses overwhelmed. Just as she thought her mind would collapse underneath her, something else gave way. She was falling before she knew what had happened, still trapped in a daze, she hadn't the will to react and just submitted herself to the sensation. The ground she knew was drawing nearer, though it was hidden from sight, but her wings would not obey. She did not fear the collision, it was expected and accepted, but with a jolt her descent was halted. Strong arms, a gentle breath upon the nape of her neck, and a timbrous, chiding voice.

"…sielle." She felt drowsiness overtake her with the knowledge that she was someplace safe. This voice which admonished her so softly lulled her anxious heart with the unspoken promise of security.

"Mm…" she murmured, allowing her eyes to slowly droop close. The exhilaration instilled in her by that unidentified summons had withdrawn the energy it had lent and she was sinking slowly away into the place of forsaken dreams.

"Asielle!" The voice was sharper now. She giggled to herself, *Lianzet sounds annoyed.*

"Must I wake you with a kiss?"

Her eyelids shot open as the echo of that remark reached her ears. *Lianzet would never say that!*

His face was close to hers, the threat of a kiss unmistakably real, and she wondered briefly if she wasn't a bit disappointed that it wasn't Lianzet. Not that she had any right to complain, most Angels never found love. Love, what would that even mean for her anyways, nobody had bothered to explain such a thing to her. As far as she knew, love didn't really exist, it was a fabled concept not grounded in her reality. And what was she doing engaging in such frivolous thoughts instead of occupying her mind with more prudent questions like where she was.

Lips as soft as velvet grazed the downy skin above her mouth.

"Snap out of it or I'll bite you," came the wicked whisper.

"I am not so unaware that I cannot stab you," she grumbled back.

He chuckled warmly, a shockingly delightful sound, pleasant as the sound of a river rolling over stone.

"Well, it seems that fiery spirit of yours cannot be doused so easily." The relief in his tone was obvious even to her frayed senses.

"Hmph. I really must stop appearing so weak in front of you."

"Why? I'm rather enjoying it." His eyes crinkled mischievously and she was struck anew by their luster. He noticed, and winked at her slyly, he seemed to notice everything, and this hyperawareness made her feel uncomfortably scrutinized. She looked away quickly, afraid of the intensity that burned deep in their depths, threatening to incinerate her. She looked anywhere but at him, at the ground speedily approaching, at the pinprick of sun-kissed moonlight evaporating into the darkness from whence they had fallen. She could hear the voice no longer, the lack of even so much as an echo made her wonder if it had only been imagined. Ahead she saw the blurred lights of many flickering candles adorning the walls of a hallowed corridor. *But why…why is this here?*

"This place…"she murmured, tentative to break the solaced silence, and afraid of what might answer her hushed voice.

"Do you know it? It seems to be an underground passage of some sort."

His feet touched lightly to the ground and he retracted his wings to fit within the confined space. She attempted to leap down but she was still firmly entrenched in his strong arms.

"Ephremael…"

"Hm?" He looked down at her impatient glare and smiled. "Have I mentioned how much I love it when you say my name?"

"You can put me down now." She said, ignoring his query.

"Hah, I'm getting so used to holding you that I hadn't even noticed." His eyes flashed to accompany his brazen smile.

"Well, that may be," she said crankily, "but put me down."

"Yes milady." He obliged, gently releasing her. "Not even a thanks for my gallantry?"

"You've done nothing deserving of my thanks." She said curtly, though her tone was benign.

It's not as though my life would ever forfeit to a fall. She started to wander down the glowing corridor but was held back by a firm hand.

"I shall go first."

He didn't need to state why, she instantly understood his reasoning. The last underground corridor they'd been privy to had been far less than welcoming. She acquiesced politely; this was one matter that she would not fight him on.

They walked on, their shadows casting eerie portraits on the walls that stained into stone like spilled ink, and left the virgin white tainted. It was as if their sins remained stamped upon the walls even after they'd long since passed. Gloomy thoughts breed in gloomy places, fostered by the desire to be known. *But what is it to be known? If knowing meant to be remembered and to be unknown meant to die…then life lay in the knowing. If Lianzet and the others are gone, then who am I known to?*

She watched the broad soldiers that led the way through this unidentifiable place with a renewed sense of curiosity tinged by fear. If all else she had come to know and love were suddenly to be no more, then what would this I'rae become to her, as the only one left that knew her? *Would I rather be nothing than be something to him?* Wouldst that she knew, but that kind of thing is never known until after it has become fact. And merely to know it imparted no control over its formation, what inevitably would be, inevitably would be. *But still, why should it be him who navigates the treacherous darkness alongside of me?* Her heart mourned for Lianzet's absence all the more, for the reassurance and stability his mere presence promised her. *Oh Lianzet, what has become of you?*

She remembered that briefest of moments when Ephremael's lips had melded with her own, and how for that instantaneous eternity, factions and war had dropped out of existence. Was there any way to make that sensibility last? Her sense of guilt was expounded by the fevered heat that tore through her body at the remembered taste of that molten moment. She had completely forgotten herself in his embrace, and that must never happen again, for forgetting was inherently dangerous. And yet, she would gladly forget all that had transpired today if only it were offered. All we are is a sequence of moments, but some of those moments she could do without. *After today, I will forget you Ephremael, I'll forget even your name, never to cross my mind again.*

As if he had heard his name as it vibrated through her thoughts he spoke.

"Why did you come this way? You must know what is hidden here?" he sounded suspicious.

How could she say it was because she'd heard a voice?

"I was merely attempting to get away from you." She said coolly.

"Of course," he said with a humorless chuckle. "What other reason could there be?"

He turned towards her with a scarily serious expression.

"If I am to protect you, it would be far easier if I knew what it was that I'm protecting you from." That was all before he turned back and continued into the passage.

A sense of timid misgiving afflicted her at keeping the truth concealed, but to hear a voice in her head that was not that of God would only serve to further prove how unlike the rest of the Angels she was. The truth would only worry him, but why should she care if he worried? She truly hated to admit it, even to herself, but she was fast becoming dependent on him. He stopped suddenly and she collided with his strong back.

"Isn't that..." he trailed off and she followed his gaze to a faded jade pedestal upon which lay a familiar looking piece of vellum.

"The Scroll...what is it doing here?" She remembered the voice that had summoned her to this place. It had known, somehow, that the Scroll was here. She wanted to forget that the Scrolls even existed, her relationship to them had ostracized her enough, at least that's how it felt to her. It seemed that the Scrolls wanted something from her, and whatever it may be it was more than she was prepared to offer. *I don't want to be singled out,* she thought, could she not pretend that she had not seen it here, and merely walk on?

Ephremael was slowly advancing towards the Scroll and she snapped out of her selfishness.

"Stop right there!" she commanded, placing her body resolutely in his path with what she hoped was a fearsome expression.

He halted and cocked an eyebrow at her.

"You think I intend to steal it?" he queried.

"Of course I do! You nearly killed me in the pursuit of it! Is that…" her heart clenched with dread, "Is that why you saved me? So that I would lead you here?" Her voice was frail and small with the silent wish that he would deny it.

He was quiet, studying her features closely, and she almost shouted at him to retort with his usual cockiness. This brooding silence frightened her, though his unpredictability was somewhat exhilarating. Just as she was about to tense herself for the battle she was certain was coming, he spoke with heavily weighted words, each one fraught with raw determination.

"You still do not trust me?"

She faltered momentarily. 'What reason have you given me to trust you?' is what she wanted to say, but it wasn't a complete truth that he'd given her no reasons. In fact, if she really were to think on it, the reasons to trust him far outweighed her reasons to not. She felt that she wished to trust him, suspicion was tiresome and she already weary.

"It…does not matter what I think of you." She said carefully. "How can an Angel ever truly trust an I'rae?"

He was clearly exasperated by this response. "Stupid, what you think is all that matters!" He took hold of her shoulders and roughly pulled her against his chest.

"Don't you get it? What more do I have to do to get my feelings across to you?" She could barely hear him over the pounding of his heart.

"I…I-" she stammered uncomfortably, her hands trapped against his chest made pushing away from him improbable.

"I thought your stubbornness alluring at first, but it's fast becoming a frustration," his breath stirred the hair on her head and she knew that he was looking down at her. "Have I not risked my life for you?"

She wanted to protest it, just as she wanted to protest all nonsensical things, but she could not hope to debate the truth. She spoke with great forethought.

"You almost certainly have ulterior motives for it, but what you say is true. You did-" she choked on the words, "save me."

"It was only right that I return the favor." He said softly.

More confused than ever, she questioned him, "When have I ever saved you?"

"Why, the very first time I saw you, and every day since."

"You…make no sense. None whatsoever." She felt at ease now that he was back to his teasing ways.

"I cannot deny that I have ulterior motives for rescuing you." He let the words hang in the air and watched her face as all past doubts were renewed. "However-I doubt they are what you suppose them to be. In fact, I am sure they have not occurred to you at all."

A fouler intention than any she could imagine? *What a horrifying notion.* Unease gnawed at her heart like a termite at rotted wood. He knew that she was in his debt, what would she do when he came to collect?

"I'm surprised that Halliel would leave the Scroll unattended, he is not the type to be so careless."

An astute observation, one that she should have made herself. She would have expected Halliel to have something so precious on his person at all times, a symbol of his right to lead, not stowed away in some forgotten passage. But then, he probably thought it was worthless, no words, no power. He'd even accused her of mistakenly fetching a decoy. Maybe he'd come to the conclusion that this scrap of virginal velum was undeserving of his protection.

"So, this one is also blank." Ephremael said as he handled the unrolled Scroll.

"That is not for you to touch!" *Why can I not focus with him around?*

"I almost killed her, over this?" His voice was quiet with a sort of enraged disbelief and she knew that he had not meant to speak out loud.

She wrested the Scroll from his obliging grasp and it shimmered gleefully at her touch. So shocked was she by this reaction that she promptly dropped it and it fell listlessly to the ground at her feet.

Ephremael stared at her incredulously before laughing lightly and stooping to pick it up.

"You're rather clumsy for an Angel, aren't you?" he chided playfully.

"Y-yes, I suppose I am." She agreed, clearly he had not seen what she had.

As she retrieved it from him her hand trembled slightly in anticipation, and it glowed fiercely as expected. As she watched in horror the golden inscriptions leapt from the Scroll and began to twist their way up her arm, tattooing words onto pearly exposed skin, leaving the Scroll as blank as everyone else supposed it to be. As she stared as if hypnotized, she couldn't keep her mind from screaming: *"No, no, NO!"* She felt invaded, slowly being taken over by this alien force to whom her personal will undoubtedly meant zilch. *This is my body, get out!* She felt like sobbing as she watched helplessly. Intricate flowing script now covered almost her entire right arm, turning it golden in hue, as stunning as Lianzet's eyes. A firm, fiery grip on her arm brought her gaze up into the perfectly contrasted turquoise turmoil of Ephremael's stare. The golden letters seemed to balk at his touch, diverging around his palm so that a blank space was left. She tried to discern the meaning behind his expression, *could he see the markings?* Perhaps she would not be so alone in her fear if at least one other could validate things as she saw them, but the fear of rejection still lingered. Would he think her an anomaly?

"What has you so frightened?" he asked softly.

"You…cannot see it." A tendril of frail disappointment crept into her subdued reply.

"What is it that I am meant to see?" he prodded.

She didn't reply verbally, merely shaking her head. *Of course he cannot see it, it is probably not even really there.*

"Asielle?"

Nobody sees these things…because they are not real. She stared at the delicate lettering wound tightly about her fingers like rings and felt helpless enough to cry at the prospect of being unable to trust her own perceptions.

"Tell me what it is you wish me to see, and I swear to you that I shall see it." His tone was almost pleading, as though asking her to let him understand her.

He is better off not understanding me, she thought miserably, *they are all better off not understanding me.* She envisioned the frozen face of Baukutet and cringed inwardly.

"You couldn't even dream the things that I see." She finally managed to muster, after several failed attempts at a suitable response.

"I cannot hope to ever understand you, then?" It was more statement than query; it is not as though there are ever definitive answers for such things.

She kind of half-smiled, wanting the conversation to be over and feeling sapped by the cloying stillness of these tomblike tunnels, but Ephremael clung to the notion.

Ephremael

"Give me permission to know you further."

A short chirping laugh that sounded flat to his ears.

"I would have you know me less, not more."

"You speak as though Lianzet were here. He is not. He is not the one who saved you; I have been the one to stand beside you. And yet, he is still foremost in your mind." He eyed her with hungry impatience, feeling as though he fought a losing battle against himself with every passing moment.

"Is there no changing this?" He asked, trying to keep the hunter's edge from coloring his words.

"When you have been a faithful friend for more than one day, then maybe you will have the right to compare yourself to Lianzet! Lianzet is not my hero only when he chooses to be!" The lethargy melted away from her eyes and a caustic bite framed her voice. She waited for an adverse reaction, a slighting word or derisive sneer but instead he offered her a knavish smile.

"Very well then, I accept the challenge." He leaned in close, eyes twinkling in the dark, illuminated from within their depths like light cast upwards from under waves. His breath was upon her ear as he whispered.

"Let's hope you're worth the effort." He nipped playfully at her tender earlobe as it flushed a conch-like pink and she withdrew from his invasive proximity as a leaping deer from a salivating wolf.

Even frightened, hers was a dreamy stare, one that he fully indulged himself in without the strangulation of guilt. *Asielle, even in this darkness you shine.* She was grasping the vellum so tightly that her hands began to shake and her fingers to twitch and he began to perceive that there was something of a trapped bird to her movements. Who would she be if he were to release her, and would he love her still?

"I hate when you stare at me so." She said petulantly, arms protectively braced in an attempt to hide her skin.

"Hm, and I hate when you hide the truth from me, so as far as I'm concerned that makes us even."

She didn't deny it, he knew that she couldn't. Whatever it was that she kept so closely guarded, she was wanting to share it, he could see that she sought an outlet. If he could but manage to convince her to share it with him, he knew it would create an inescapable bond between them. He did not even make an attempt to reign in the furious jealousy that swept a course through him at the thought it was more than likely that she kept this secret only to share it with Lianzet. Physically, he was no match for Lianzet, that he well knew, but when it came to winning the love of a woman, he had yet to lose. And with stakes this high, he surely could not afford to.

She was rubbing her arm vigorously, as if to rub the skin itself off.

"If I didn't know better, I'd think you were cold." He said pointedly.

She abruptly stopped the restless movement.

"To be cold…is just one of the many things I can never feel." Almost mournful was her tone.

"I am quite certain the humans would envy that." He inched closer. "I can warm you, regardless…"

"Let us leave here. Clearly, the cramped quarters have afflicted you with delusions." She snapped.

"If your delusions are to match mine, than clearly we must linger longer." He countered.

"Whatever your delusions may be, I want no part in them." She replied coolly.

As if you don't know, that in this moment and every moment hence, the only wish of my deluded heart is to lay claim to your lips once more. Time and time again until I've branded you with my lust and made your body sing my name. My name, not Lianzet's. He wondered if she was merely being coy, but soon concluded that even knowing the meaning of the word was beyond her. *She's almost too innocent.* He mused, feeling almost guilty for his acts of ardor towards her. How unfair that she should fuel his desires so adeptly without any awareness that she was doing so. What would it take to have her mirror this feverish hunger? Desperate to curtail his cravings before they manifested as actions, he returned to the fear that had been recently reflected in her eyes, a reaction to something he could not see. An idea cast faint illumination through his mind.

"Asielle," How familiar and precious that name had become to him, and in such an impossibly short time. "The things that you see, do not think that they are not real simply because I cannot see them. I too, have seen things that defy explanation. I was guided to you by one such mirage." He paused at the remembrance of that logic defying creature before asking gently, "Is it that same woman that appears to you now?"

She started, clearly having forgotten that he was present for that bewildering event. *Am I so very forgettable to her?*

"I wish I could say it were, at least there was some sense to be made of that apparition."

That look of abject panic that had fled across her face upon contact with the Scroll, how could mere scraps of hide render such fear? And why could he not see this as she had that less than Angel? *I would gladly destroy those Scrolls if it meant releasing her from her terror.* Seized by that sudden impulse he reached for Asielle, who characteristically backed away.

"Asielle, give me the Scroll." He ordered.

"Why? What is your intent?" she seemed exhausted, her spark partially extinguished and fiery tongue dimmed.

"I intend to destroy it." He stated simply, even knowing that she would not believe him.

She laughed unexpectedly.

"Destroy it? The very objects that we both risked our lives over? Truly, you must be delusional to even suggest such a thing."

He persisted.

"These Scrolls have brought nothing but misery to all involved, and for what? They cannot even be read."

An expression that he could not fathom irked her fair countenance and he hastened to add: "And even if they could be read, there is nothing that they might say to justify all that has been done in their name."

The teasings of tears was evident at the corner of her lucent eyes once more, though he could not begin to contemplate why. *Why is it that I can say nothing that does not cause her pain?*

"Am I wrong in thinking thus?" he queried.

"Are you wrong," she repeated. "You must be wrong, you are I'rae." He waited, aware that she was only musing to herself, and clearly did not have the answer.

"This war…would not cease with the existence of the Scrolls, they'd soon find another reason to fight." She said quietly. "Though I do not understand why they must."

"Those Scrolls, they believe them to hold enough power to end this feud once and for all. For such a prize, they would fight until Heaven itself is destroyed."

"Surely even Olucard could not wish for that!"

"Not even I know the depths that my brother is willing to sink to." Ephremael said with some disdain. "He is so far lost as to be almost demon."

He expected horror, or even faint pity but she showed no such reactions. Instead she appeared further mired in thought, cradling the slightly battered Scroll close to her chest.

"With both Scrolls…I could end this war?"

"The other Scroll is with my brother. You cannot hope to take it from him."

"If it means an end to this fighting, I'll find a way." Her voice quavered, betraying her strong spirit.

"It is a foolish thing to risk your life for, when there's no guarantee that they can even be read once reunited." He was angry at himself for planting such a dangerous suggestion in such a quietly pliant mind. She was dispersing like ash, willingly swirled by wind, not solid enough to cling to, yet cling he did. If there were not someone there to cement her reality, would she simply float away? Without a shared stake in fantasy, would her fragile sense of self crumble? And if she were to crumble, what act of God would suffice to piece her back together again? Or perhaps she'd simply remain forever fragmented, torn asunder by inner uncertainties. Would she then intrigue him so? Stray longing escaped from betwixt parted lips. The suffering was at an end, brought to shame by bended knee. He shook off his thoughts like a hound frees the water from its fur. It was of no import what could, should, or might have been. What mattered was that intrigue him she did, though he still could not say why, nor what it meant, if indeed it meant anything at all.

"They can be read." She said so softly as to be nearly

indistinguishable from breath.

"What was that?" He was irritated now, against his wishes.

She rephrased. "And if they could be read?"

"Then God save us all." He snickered dryly.

Should they be read, was the real question. Which would bring salvation, to read or to destroy, if either offered any redemption.

The ground above crackled and roared, stirring the stillness of introspection into a raging torrent of fear. Chunks of rock long forgotten by the world above came down on their heads in a relentless shower. The cracks were so deep the moonlight shone through, illuminating the fissures into mosaics of light. The pounding seemed unnaturally loud, magnified by the quiet of the depths. Ephremael braced his wings against the close walls, a feathery shield protecting Asielle from the falling rubble. They grew tattered with pierced holes as the avalanche continued, large chunks of ceiling threatening to crush them underneath their weight. Specks of moonlight fell like freckles upon Asielle's upturned face. He scowled, she was just asking for a face full of rock shards. What could possibly be going on up above to cause this? Layers of earth and stone undisturbed for countless millennium wiped out within a brief sequence of minutes. The roof above turned to windblown sky, stars shining close enough to touch, but near to nothing, overwhelmed by the moon's luminance.

They emerged from the darkness with well-practiced caution, and then quickly wished to disappear back inside as if scared of their own shadows.

Giants roamed the halls of Heaven.

Asielle

No…why? How can this be? And as if her question had been heard, in flew the answer; a giant supported on all sides by six I'rae, struggling to keep the massive creature aloft despite their preternatural strength. Behind them the silhouettes of many wings in flight, beating in unison as they lurched awkwardly towards their destination, bearing their cumbersome loads. An entire army of giants was descending, their heavy steps turning the ground beneath them to naught more than dust and fond memories.

She scanned the blackened skies of Heaven, moon blotted out by multitudes of wings, searching for that one familiar face that she was so used to appearing in her times of strife. Even the face of Halliel would be a welcome sight now. Yet the one familiar face she could find was that of Ephremael beside her, Darklight humming in camaraderie with its fellow blades.

They could not hope to fight off this many. As the giants swung their massive limbs, adept at destruction and the towers of Itsukuenel toppled to the ground besmirched by craterous footprints that had no right to tread there, they cowered behind a pillar, shocked into inaction.

In her clasped hand the Scroll twitched as if begging to be read, though she knew it was only from her clutching onto it so tightly. They more she held it, the more she felt certain that something like that was not meant to be read. Even if words are birthed onto parchment for no other purpose but to be read, still it seemed, as inaccessible as they were, that the power held by those finely scribed words was somehow forbidden, as forbidden as her ability to read them. And if she were to read them, not knowing what their purpose, and all of Heaven collapsed around her…No, even in this predicament it was eternally not worth the risk.

"We've got to leave." Came Ephremael's close and urgent whisper. "There's nothing we can do."

She knew what he really meant.

"Abandon Heaven? No, I-I cannot."

"When there's no possibility of victory, retreat is the only option. I won't have you die here."

"As one who's already abandoned your home and your kin, I wouldn't expect you to understand." She quipped. "For me, this is my only home. I know nothing else."

Every blow to these hallowed halls, every fracture in the sacred stone was as a blow to her very core, as if pieces of her were being smashed, as if it was her blood that seeped from every crack, instead of simply dust. The Holy City was creaking under the load of so many giants, and it began to tilt slightly, sending Asielle sliding into Ephremael, who kept his balance deftly.

"What would you do, take on this army alone?" he eyed her seriously. "I would follow, but our deaths will not save Heaven."

She knew this was true, but even so, how could she not try? It was then that a horrible screeching tore into her ears, rippling down her spine in horrid waves. The sound made her want to retch, even had she not known what it was. They'd been spotted by a Dervish Imp. Riding high atop the towering shoulders of a lumbering giant, it pointed through the shadows at where they crouched, whirring back and forth in frenzied movements. The corresponding giant brought down its fist with an impact that sent them reeling even as they lunged to safety.

"Well, well, now what do we have here? A filthy deserter and his sin." Sneered an I'rae come to investigate. "I'll finish you both off. Olucard will surely praise me."

"He's mine." Interrupted a second, more sinister voice as a whip curled itself around the I'rae's feet and yanked him off-balance.

"Anguilla." Ephremael growled as a female I'rae melted from

shadow into view. She reeked of an almost alien, raw sensuality, so strong
as to be revolting. Yet she was alluring in an obvious, crude fashion. As
Asielle glanced from this serpentine beauty to Ephremael, who would have
had his hackles up if he'd had any, a disturbing suspicion entered her mind.
Could they...? Not that she knew how to finish that thought, she felt the
seductive prowess of this I'rae as strongly as she imagined glittering fangs
of Darklight hidden behind her smirk, but just what it meant to be a
seductress, or to be seduced, she had only the vaguest notion.

Anguilla slithered closer, stepping callously on the outstretched
wing of her angered comrade.

"Ah, Ephremael, what a pitiful sight you are." She clucked her
tongue at Ephremael's ragged wings before lasering in on Asielle, equally
disheveled and seemingly formed of dust.

"Really, Ephre, I'm beginning to question your tastes. You'd
choose this...dishrag of a girl over me? Over your own dear brother?"

Ephremael laughed harshly.

"There is nothing further from 'dear' to me than my brother."

Anguilla pouted becomingly. "I thought myself at least a little dear
to you, Ephre. And yet you go and do something so foolish." Her next
words were carefully calculated. "Yet thanks to your foolishness, we've
successfully infiltrated Heaven." Her face morphed into a menacing mask.
"Yes, it's all thanks to Ephre that this," she waved her arms in sweeping
fashion at the chaos behind her, "was all possible." Seeing Asielle's distrust
her mouth formed a surprised O and she raised her hand over it in mock
disbelief.

"Oh! Ephre I get it now! This was all a part of your plan, wasn't it
you clever boy?" She drew closer to Ephremael. "You knew I was following
you, didn't you? You led me right into Heaven on purpose! Oh, Ephre...!"
She flung her arms languorously around Ephremael's neck. "Did you do
this so that we could be together? Mm I shall have to reward you, then."
She leaned up to give Ephremael a kiss as Asielle watched with a mixture of
utter shock and horror. Ephremael was so intent on Asielle's reaction that
Anguilla managed to steal a kiss and smiled slyly at Asielle.

"So you see, honey, Ephre has only ever had eyes for me. Why, he
follows me around like a wee puppy dog. He betrayed you." She smiled up
at a stiffened Ephremael. "You always taste so...delicious."

"You..." Asielle managed to choke out, flushed with fury.

"Asielle..." Ephremael's voice was dangerously low.

"No! Don't talk to me, you...you!" she meant to sound enraged
but her voice trembled with tears instead.

"Oh look, she's going to cry, how cute." Anguilla sneered. "What a
pathetic, sniveling wretch. Really Ephre, how <u>do</u> you put up with her?"

"Silence you miserable slattern!" Ephremael snapped upon seeing the anguish in Asielle's eyes and managed to nick Anguilla's neck with his blades before she flitted agilely out of range.

"Ah, a love bite, I do so love it when you're rough." Anguilla said, wiping the blood off with one finger as it trickled down into her décolletage.

"Asielle, don't listen to her, this farce of a woman knows only lies. I would never, could never betray you."

"And yet, we would not have made it into Heaven without him." Anguilla interjected, as she admired her glistening fingernails.

"Will you shut up?!" Ephremael flung one of his blades at her face, shearing off a lock of her midnight blue tresses and scarring her perfectly matte cheek.

"Don't be careless, dear. You should really take better care of your things." Anguilla said calmly, retrieving Ephremael's blade and twirling it about in her palm.

"Enough. Stop toying with them, Anguilla, we have all of Heaven to conquer." The first I'rae interrupted, having managed to stagger to his feet.

"I will say when it's enough!" Anguilla hissed. "Go and make yourself useful elsewhere."

"But—" the I'rae protested.

"Go!" she boomed and he skittered off, casting irate glances back at them.

"You. Giant." She commanded to the placid mountain behind her. "Crush the girl. We have no need of her now."

The giant grunted in reply but made no move. Anguilla sighed, exasperated, and pointed at Asielle. "Her. Kill. Now!"

Seemingly comprehending, the giant's limbs cracked like avalanches as it positioned itself to strike at Asielle.

"Leave her, Anguilla. I'm the one you want." Ephremael protested, blocking the giant's way.

"This is your last chance, Ephremael. Your last chance to prove your loyalty to the cause, to Olucard. Smash her smug little face into pieces so tiny they can never be scooped up, or be smashed along with her. I tire of this little game, stop playing hard to get." She twirled her hair around her pointy fingers nonchalantly.

"You should go with her." Asielle said flatly, feeling strangely apathetic inside.

"Asielle…"

"Go home Ephremael!" Asielle shouted, projecting her voice at him like a missile, sending him sliding backwards.

"Asielle, don't do this. Let me help you."

"I do not need the help of a traitor. Just, just stay away from me. Go back where you belong!" She attacked the giant recklessly, not really caring if she won as tears came streaming down her cheeks in silent waves.

"I belong with you! Surely you can see that!" Ephremael joined her in the fight as Anguilla watched languidly.

"How very touching." She commented. "I had wanted to save you, Ephre. You're such a…fine specimen. So very beautiful and yet," she almost seemed wistful as she paused, "so stupid. To choose her over me is surely some form of insanity."

She glanced at Ephremael, slashing away at the giant's thick skin.

"You are sure you cannot be tempted to change your mind?"

"Call off your giants and leave, Anguilla." Ephremael shouted as his remaining blade plunged into the giant's molten eye, causing the creature to roar with infuriated pain. "I will <u>never</u> choose you."

"Have it your way."

Anguilla's whip snaked through the air, its barbed tongue digging into Asielle's pale, vulnerable flesh like fangs. She yelped in surprised pain, her attack on the giant interrupted mid-strike. The giant, slow-witted as it was, was not dull enough to miss the opportunity and swung at her, connecting with a sickening thud that sent her spinning into ground.

"Asielle!" Ephremael attempted to move to her side but was blocked by a sneering Anguilla.

"You get to watch her die, Ephre, and I guarantee that I will make her suffer!" she cracked her whip at his feet, further riling him, and seemingly taking pleasure in his increasing distress. The giant raged towards Asielle, who righted herself and barely managed to parry the onslaught of blows it reaped upon her cowed body. Ephremael tried again to come to her aid, but Anguilla inserted herself in his way, whip grazing his arm and sending flecks of silver blood flying through the dawn. Ephremael's lone blade flashed as he engaged Anguilla in combat, his furious blows benefitting from the strength loaned by anger, but his attention compromise so that she easily sidestepped and escaped unscathed.

Asielle sang until her throat was numb and notes jagged, but nothing more than common battle spells emerged, aid enough for one giant, perhaps, but the skirmish had attracted the attention of several of the roaming beasts who were now staggering towards them.

Why? Why forsake me now? Asielle wondered. *The one time my difference would be welcomed you abandon me?* She tried to focus her energy as she had against Halliel but to no avail. Forever a disobedient gift, it seemed.

Anguilla's whip struck at Ephremael's tattered left wing, constricting around it, crushing feathers and sinew, grounding him. He bravely fought on, growling like a beast as she darted nimbly about, wearing him down slowly. A second giant arrived on the scene, its fist like a sledgehammer as it struck at Asielle and just barely missed. The first giant flung a slab of a collapsed column at her, and a shard separated and pierced through her shoulder as she winced with pain.

"Leave her be!" Ephremael bellowed, charging without forethought at the giant as it swung a fallen tree at him. His speed was only minutely affected by the loss of his wings and he managed to evade, landing a successful stab to the giant's craggy foot which only served to infuriate it further. The dagger stuck, resisting his efforts to free it and leaving him unarmed.

"Oh, what will you do now?" Anguilla taunted as Ephremael avoided the giant's outraged counters.

Asielle glanced at the two blades in her hands; loathe to give either up but well knowing that now was not the time to be choosy about one's allies.

"Ephremael!" she shouted, decision reached.

"Here!" she hurled her left-hand blade at him as Anguilla's whip stretched out to intercept and knock it off-course. It was a tense moment as both raced for the blade, and Asielle glanced away, unable to bear the tension.

Anguilla's angry yelp testified to the victor, and Asielle looked to see Ephremael triumphantly wielding a blade of Heaven just as naturally as he had one of Shadowlight. Of course, blades care not for allegiance, even magical ones, so it should not have been so surprising a sight. Her attention was drawn back to the giants and she lost track of Ephremael. Adjusting her battle strategy to suit a singular blade drastically reduced her lethality, even with all the strength of her song it was a struggle to fend the giants off, let alone inflict any damage. Most of her energy spent in defending she began to grow weary and sloppy, taking several direct hits.

She continued to fight with increasing desperation, occasionally landing a successful strike until finally she wore down the first giant enough to deliver a fatal blow. The giant screeched in protest as it tumbled over, eyes slowly growing dim as its fiery life-force dissipated. The second giant lumbered over its fallen comrade without care, lurching at Asielle with a deep bellow. As she evaded it, she felt a burning sensation in her side, and looking down saw a gaping wound, and sticking out of it, coated in her blood, was one of Ephremael's daggers.

Turning in shock she saw Ephremael and Anguilla engaged in combat, seemingly oblivious. The giant's heavy fist connected with her ribs, sending her flying into a nearby pile of rubble. As she achingly got to her feet, vision blurring slightly, she could faintly make out Ephremael fighting his way towards her. She staggered away from him, his dagger still stuck deep in her flesh, and he caught sight of it with alarmed dismay.

"Asielle, no, you can't think that I—"

"You've done it before." She sputtered; blood caking her speech as the Sea Dragon scale glowed fiercely, fighting to maintain her consciousness.

Anguilla took advantage of his distraction and her whip wound itself tight about his neck, drawing blood as she yanked him back towards her.

"How dare you ignore me, Ephre. I won't have you looking at other women!" she jerked on the whip and Ephremael fell flat on his back, struggling to cut the vine-like weapon and grazing his neck with each failed attempt. He would die, the battle was over. A group of giants appeared, and Asielle faced them with false bravado, knowing that her battle, too, was done. This time, nobody was coming to save her, she would go down with Heaven.

She wept, fondly remembering the life she'd led before this all began, the adventures with Lianzet, conversations with Baukutet, midnight rides on the Stars, even the arguments with Halliel seemed precious to her now, now that all those moments stood to be lost forever. And there, in those tears, in those displaced emotions, she found her song. She found it and released it as the last time she'd be free to hear it. Everything would end in death, but she had been born in song and meant to die in it. That primal, mysterious power coated everything, and the world seemed to glow bright in violet hues, and time slowed to a crawl. Like a strange dance the giants slowly waded through the song like water, pushed about by its ripples, and crushed beneath its waves. The song began to churn with the ugly bitterness of loss, and the giants began to disintegrate into light. into blinding light, just like her mind. She struggled to hold on, but the song was so very draining. *You've done all you can,* it soothed, *rest now.* She slipped in and out of awareness.

So, I am to die. she thought. *How very…strange.* Perhaps, in the eternal embrace of death, she would finally find the peace that so eluded her in life. Perhaps, in becoming nothing, she would mean something. Perhaps.

Perhaps.

Disquieting void, vast nothingness and an irritating hum reverberating through the caliginous black, becoming the black. *All things to black. All things, here, to black. Black exists in all things. Black exists in you. You are black. You.*

Whispers in the void. *Is this…death?* Faint sparks lit up the noir, only to sputter agonizingly out, leaving the world even darker than before, having stolen the promise of light, of hope.

The light is never enough, breathed the dark. *It can offer you nothing. Become one with all, for all is black.* The Cimmerian landscape trembled around her senses, and she felt darkness coat her lungs as she inhaled, though she felt without body.

Yes…she thought wearily. *Yes, I shall stay here. Nothing can reach me, I can reach nobody, just to dream is all there is.* The darkness deepened, far beyond the color black, into the atramentous bleakness before creation, and she flowed willingly with it. All awareness slipped quietly away, as the black consumed her fading light.

Goodbye…Lianzet. She thought.

"ASIELLE!" a voice yelled from somewhere beyond the dark. She endeavored to listen, even as the black placated any desires she had to be free.

"ASIELLE!" it came again, tearing through the darkness and allowing slivers of light to infiltrate.

Whose voice is that? She wondered drowsily. *Who calls me? Leave me be.*

"ASIELLE!" the voice snapped, and the dark grew less stygian. Irritated, she swam towards the voice, willing it to be quiet and allow her to drift away but it came again, more insistent, and with a final push she emerged into consciousness, leaving the black behind.

Boots of opalescent Uthicon encircled her, their glorious shine at first all that she could see. She tried to move but found her body unresponsive, too badly mangled to heed her summons. Shifting her eyes she made out the contour of lambent golden wings, backlit by a fuming sun. Squinting, she tried to correct for her obvious error in vision, no Angel possessed golden wings. She tried to remember what Anguilla had worn, for surely this was she, come to gloat over her conquered foe.

"Alfuen lensbar (take her)." said an unfamiliar voice in the ancient tongue, unused since God first reigned, though all Angels knew it.

Strong arms lifted her battered body, and she could see now her rescuers. Or, sort of see them in any case, they shone with such refulgent light she could scarce make out identifying features, an aquiline nose, smoldering eyes of faceted sapphire piercing through the dense halo of golden rays. These were Angels, surely, but what manner of Angel she could not say. She had never seen their like before and felt sincerely humbled, so in awe was she of their inherent splendor. These beings were the closest to God that she had felt in many millennium and she felt a bit like a wayward child come home.

As the magnificent creature bore her upwards in flight, she surveyed the shredded landscape below, the ground riven asunder by the stampeding feet of countless giants and fraught with the stains of conflict. She spotted Anguilla's body, slumped against a fractured column, her eyes rolled grotesquely back in her head, her jaw hanging open, protruding out of its socket and perforating through her skin. Asielle felt qualmish, and her eyes roved around the carnage until she espied Ephremael's lacerated form, strung out among the ruin, glorious even in his disarray. She felt a stirring in her breast, perhaps more excruciating than her corporeal wounds, despite any imagined transgressions on his part. As her eyes flitted away and the ground receded further from view, a spurt of movement caught her attention. Ephremael shifted with agonizing slowness, he yet lived. Decumbent on his back, his gleaming eyes shone up at her as his lips aspired to produce sound.

"We have to go back for him!" she found herself shouting to her rescuers, who paid her no heed. She attempted wriggling free, intent on retrieving her one-time companion, but her body still staunchly refused to obey and Ephremael grew ever further away.

"As...le." She thought she heard him cry, his voice tossed carelessly about by the wind and the whooshing of wings. Any inkling of resentment she'd harbored towards him was eclipsed by her desire to save even one soul from the carnage of the day's event and she again appealed to her saviors.

"Please, please, you must rescue him!" the numinous beings gave no assurance of comprehension.

As she was borne away into a sky so blue as to seem blind to the sanguinary and catalytic battle that had ensued, Ephremael expended the last of his strength in calling after her, not knowing if she heard.

"Asielle...I love you."

ABOUT THE AUTHOR

Nina lives in a cute rental by the ocean in the Puget Sound with her boyfriend Jon, three adorable cats and a turd of a bird. She has been writing diligently since elementary school and used to dream of being an author. Nina is a lover of nature and animals of all shapes and sizes and regularly contributes to charities. This is her first book, intended as the first in a three-part series.